You Have a Kind Face

Reflections on a Firefighter's Journey

You Have a Kind Face

Kind Face

Reflections on a Firefighter's Journey

Joel Simmons

Halo
PUBLISHING
INTERNATIONAL

Halo Publishing International
7550 WIH-10 #800, PMB 2069,
San Antonio, TX 78229

First Edition, May 2024
ISBN: 978-1-63765-597-9
Library of Congress Control Number: 2024906585

Halo Publishing International is a self-publishing company that publishes adult fiction and non-fiction, children's literature, self-help, spiritual, and faith-based books. We continually strive to help authors reach their publishing goals and provide many different services that help them do so. We do not publish books that are deemed to be politically, religiously, or socially disrespectful, or books that are sexually provocative, including erotica. Halo reserves the right to refuse publication of any manuscript if it is deemed not to be in line with our principles. Do you have a book idea you would like us to consider publishing? Please visit www.halopublishing.com for more information.

For my wife and partner, Laura. You were always in my corner.

For my sons Connor and Noble. The most fun I ever had in my life was raising my two boys.

To Josh, who invited me to join him to apply in the first place, and Jeff, who became my instant friend the day we met.

Contents

Foreword   15

Introduction   17

"You Have a Kind Face"   18
What Did People Do Before the 911 System?
Did Everyone Just Die??   20

Chapter 1
Station 23, Fresh Off the Farm   23

Maggot Samples   24
"Forget That Fire!"   25
How Much Can Happen in a Night?   26
Man vs. Train   29
Like a Horror Movie   32
So This Is Christmas   34
If You Don't Want to Be in Trouble,
Don't Go Where Trouble Lives   36
Kicking Field Goals   39
The Hispanic Panic   42
Overall General Impression   44

Chapter 2
Station 34   49

Russian Roulette   49
Fries with That?   51
Like a Glove   52
Castor Oil Fixes It   55
Like a Dog   56
Guns Ablazing   58
I Don't Blame the Father   60
The Only English He Knows?   62
Don't Disturb His Spirit   64
My Worst Call   66
Station 32   70
"He's Not Going In"   72
Leaving 34's   74

Chapter 3
Station 26   81

Old Lady in Bed   82
We Need a Backboard   85
Bag O'Cash   87
The Fiery Rat   88
Find the Hose Line   90
Dead Plug   94
Idiot Husband   97
Pray Without Ceasing   98
Flipping Out   99
"Is This Guy Serious?"   101

Chapter 4
Leaving HFD   103

Teach?   105
Pine Mountain   107
Ice Storm and the Beginning of the End   112

Chapter 5
New Braunfels Fire Department   115

Raging River on Geronimo Creek   117
2002 Flood   124
Tailgate Trauma   125
Man vs. Train: Part Two   128
Merry Christmas   130
Double Tap   131
HFD Comes Calling   132

Chapter 6
Station 9   135

Depressed Nation   137
"You da man!"   139
61 Riesner   140
Unknown Problem   142
$10,000   145
Street People   147
Violent Way to Go   149
505 Hogan   151
The Woods   152

Happy New Year 153
Roaches, Rodents, and Such 154

Chapter 7
Station 77 157

Save My Dog 158
Potato Babies 160
The Munchies 162
Selfish 163
Excuses 164
Bubbles in the Blood 165
Choice? 166
No Room 167
Ship Fire 169
"Murder Cleaners" 170
Field Amputation 171
"Prepare for a Lawsuit" 172
"Good Thing Y'All Didn't Drop Me" 174
First Official Complaint 175
$40 Bra 176
Crepitus 177
Hurricane Rita 179

Chapter 8
On to Rescue 183

High IQ 185
Tour Bus 185
Downtown Train 186

"Learn How to Drive"   188
Crane Collapse   190
Greens Bayou   192
Double DOA   194

Chapter 9
28's   197

A Different Side of Town   199
Always Check   200
"Is This Some Kind of Prank?"   201
"We Was Hoopin'"   202
Oh, the Irony   202
"I'm Still So Drunk"   203

Chapter 10
On to 41's   207

Ambulance 41 and Coke Street   208
Neglect   209
Barking Mad   211
Scammers   212
Miscellaneous   214

Chapter 11
Bush IAH   217

ARFF Slug   217
ARFF Runs   218
Nose, Gear Up   219

Chapter 12
Looking Back   223

Opinions on 911 EMS System   224

Postscript   227

About Joel Simmons   231

Foreword

From the first time I met Joel some twenty years ago, I was keenly aware of how totally different he was from the other firemen I worked with. Most fireman are not deep thinkers. Philosophy and deep perspectives simply go beyond the scope of how we think. That's not to say that we're stupid or uneducated. We are simply good men and women who are less inclined to ponder and more likely to react and charge ahead. Our lessons in life are learned through trial and error.

What stood out to me about Joel was the fact that everything he did was carried out in a way that strived for improvement. There was a way he went about his day that was planned and thoughtful. I was a young fireman when I initially met Joel, and I took notice of these things. His time was never wasted watching TV, outside of his insatiable love for *The Curse of Oak Island* and anything to do with treasure hunting. You could set your watch to his routine and regimen. Every minute of his day was precious.

His down time was spent reading ancient scholars and poets. Even his naps had a purpose, which was to give him strength for later in the day. He gave meticulous attention to details, even down to marking on paper every set of his workout. No matter what he was doing, there was a routine. It never mattered what everyone else was doing or not doing; Joel was going to do it right.

Over these past twenty years, we both grew as men, and our careers intertwined at the beginning, the middle, and the end. That initial version of Joel I met never changed. He was then, and continues to be now, a father, husband, fireman, and friend. The one you call when you need something and the one who carries it all without complaint.

Joel is uniquely qualified to write a book about the fire service. His perspective comes from a place of genuine honesty and care. The faces, sites, and smells all have the authenticity of a man meticulous enough to routinely document it all, down to the last detail. It has been an honor to be a part of so many chapters in this life, and maybe even a story or two.

Anthony Bonifazi
March 2024

Introduction

I started out simply wanting to write down my experiences because I wished my children and grandchildren to know what their grandfather did for a living. Being a firefighter in a major city is not a normal job, and most people find the stories interesting.

A couple of years before he passed away, I interviewed my grandfather about his childhood on the family farm. He grew up barefoot, picking cotton and hunting hogs deep in the Sabine River bottoms of East Texas, and his stories fascinated me. I wish I knew those stories his father could have told, and that was the main reason I wanted to put down on paper my stories. In my opinion, too much precious family history is lost.

A word to other firefighters who may read this: Because I know how the fire service is, I realize that half of you will be positive and appreciate this book, and the other half will be jealous, petty, and dismissive and will ask, "Who does he think he is? I have better stories and more dangerous exploits." To answer your question, **I don't think I am anyone special at all.** I simply put pen to paper to record some of the things I experienced, and I encourage all of you to do the same.

I also want to address observations made in this book regarding race and culture. In today's society, it seems to be taboo to even mention the cultural differences between the Black, White, Hispanic, Asian, and Middle Eastern communities, but there are differences, and serving each of them allows one to observe these unique characteristics. And that is exactly what is in this book—observations based on my own experiences. If a racial slur is used in the story, it is because that is what was said by actual people on the scene. Nothing has been added nor taken away. The streets of Houston are NOT nice and most certainly not politically correct.

"You Have a Kind Face"

That is what she told me as we were taking care of her. I think the look of surprise on my face shocked her as she said it to me. A kind face? Not that I am a mean person, but it is just that most people have told me I look serious most of the time. I am usually anything but serious around my friends, but the "business" look is usually people's first impression of me.

As a young man, someone once told me that he believed there was a constant conflict in my heart. A struggle to put things I observed into some category that made sense to what should be normal and what should be considered wrong. Maybe that is true, but I have never had someone tell me I possessed a kind face. It was probably one of the better compliments I have been given.

On TV, people who claim to be experts think they know what is going on out in the streets of America, but they have no clue because most of their information is second- or thirdhand. To know, to really know, you need to go into these people's homes, attics, cars, hotel rooms, and apartments. You need to breathe the same cigarette-smoke-filled air, smell the rot and stink of poverty, and hear the sane and insane reasons people use to try to justify what they do.

Any fireman or cop out there can tell you more and probably better stories than mine. I can only relate to what I have witnessed. My friends and wife sometimes do not believe me when I tell them things that I have seen, so lately I have just kept quiet about most of it. "War" stories get old to some people. I don't know; maybe this book is therapy for me.

My biggest problem with riding on the ambulance—and probably why I grew to hate the ambulance—is because of what I faced most when I arrived on the scene. People not taking care of themselves and wanting someone else, like the government, to take care of the most simple things for them. Many firefighters just shrug it off and chalk it up to job security. I tried that—I really did—but I could not stop the frustration that I felt for people who just seem to be occupying space in America and not adding any benefit to our society. That whole trying-to-put-things-in-a-right-or-wrong-category thing. Call it a character flaw, one of many, but I just could not, not care. I *do* care, and that seems to be the root of my frustration. On calls that were actual emergencies, when I was allowed to do what I am trained to do and not babysit, I enjoyed the adrenaline shot I got from "go time" and the satisfaction that comes from actually helping a person in need.

What Did People Do Before the 911 System? Did Everyone Just Die??

The answer, of course, is no. Did some people die? On the most serious calls, of course, some people died because people die every day. The other 95 percent of the calls are complete nonsense; people in the old days took care of themselves, their neighbors, and their families. How did we get to a system and a state in this country that a member of the family needs to go to the doctor for severe abdominal pain, but the rest of the family does not want to take him because the Houston Rockets are playing? "Just call 911; they gotta take him" is what the patient told me his family said. How did we get here? Is the emergency 911 system becoming just another form of welfare?

The reader needs to remember that these are the runs that stand out in my memory simply because they were not "normal" runs. At the busy stations I worked, for every twelve to fifteen runs I made in a shift, one or maybe two were real emergencies. The other ten to twelve were earaches, calls for Band-Aids or tampons, street people who were cold or hungry, pregnant women needing a ride even though there were three cars in the driveway, colds, minor fevers, elderly people whom the family just wanted gone for a few days, illegal immigrants who think *el norte* is the home of the free ride to the free doctor, and, of course, home-care nurses who called so they could take the rest of the day off. People who want aspirin, have toothaches, and need toothbrushes call 911, as do people whose coworker threw up. But because our great city is so scared of being sued, we haul every one of them to the ER if they want to go. ALL OF THEM. And people wonder why emergency rooms are so crowded all of the time.

I'm jaded, right? All is not lost though. I keep a quote from David Donovan's *Once A Warrior King* close to my heart.

> *There are people of every sex and station and they yearn to be challenged to a cause. They will always be looking for that wrong to right, that ill to cure, that song to sing; and there will always be those who will go to arms in aid of the helpless and the downtrodden. Ignoring the political issues of the moment, these people will champion the weak and the poor in the face of evil and tyranny. And no matter what the outcome, in their romantic hearts they will keep secret, if secret it must*

be, that they are better men for having held
that lamp next to the golden door.

Trying to be a lamp holder, I think, is what helps me keep the conflict in my heart from growing out of control.

Chapter 1

Station 23, Fresh Off the Farm

My first assignment was to Fire Station 23 located near Lawndale and Broadway on the Houston Ship Channel. At the time, I lived in Clear Lake, and I chose 23's because it was somewhat close to where I lived. (As a sidenote, stations are referred to as 23's, 34's, etc. This is not a form of plural, but rather it is to show possession—as in, "That fire station is Engine Company 23's firehouse.")

I didn't think about being a firefighter until one day my best friend Josh said, "Hey, I'm applying to HFD. Do it with me." I said okay, and that was honestly all the thought I gave to it.

Going into the fire service, I knew I was going to see people as they died and right after they died, but I have to admit the number of dead people I made on scenes surprised me. (In the fire service, arriving at a scene is called "making" a scene.) Going to do CPR, making suicides and fatalities of all kinds became very much just part of the job. I was nudged in this direction the night I graduated from the academy. On the way to my Aunt Missy's house in Pasadena, for a celebration party, we passed right by

Engine 23 and a deformed, mangled body in the middle of Loop 610. Before I had even reported to 23's, I "made" a fatality with them. I found out the next morning that the victim was a female who tried crossing the loop and, needless to say, did not make it.

Maggot Samples

My first dead body that I got up close and personal with was a male of unknown age upstairs in a garage apartment. It was several days before anyone noticed him missing, but the telltale flies on the window and faint smell on the outside gave it away, so neighbors called it in. Opening the door to the stairway brought a burst of rot and stench that only confirmed the suspicion. I was proud of myself for not barfing on the way up or for the entire time. What we found was what, in my rookie mind, I thought was a Black male who had been there for several days in the Houston heat. I later learned it was indeed a White male, as flesh has a habit of turning black during the process of decay. The body was bloated and festering with maggots and flies. I was thankful we did not have to do anything with it; this was for HPD and the coroner now.

Outside, while waiting for my partner to finish his record, another one of the crew came up to me and told me that the police needed maggot samples. I was the rookie, so it fell to me. My first thought was that I hoped I wouldn't puke the second time I approached the body. But then

I caught a slight smile on my partner's face and knew they were messing with me. My laugh was one of relief.

"Forget That Fire!"

We were called to the scene of an automobile-bicycle accident just a couple of blocks from the station. A crowd had gathered around, and the truck had a small fire burning under the hood. My engineer and I went to open the hood and put out the fire while the captain and my best friend went to look in the ditch to which people were pointing. He and I got the hood up and were putting out the small flames with a carbon-dioxide extinguisher when we heard our captain yell, "Forget that fire! We got a kid with a split head down here!"

The truck had hit another car, which then hit a ten-year-old boy and threw him and his bike into the ditch; the bones of his skull were very visible to the horrified crowd. We immediately assisted with placing the kid on a backboard (spine board), putting a C-collar (cervical-spine immobilization device) on him, and bandaging the wound as best we could while the ambulance pulled up and the stretcher was wheeled over to us. This was what is called a "load-and-go" situation—no time is spent on the scene; you just get to the nearest ER as fast as possible. Having the mother of the child on the scene, wailing and screaming, did not help.

I have noticed cultural differences in how different ethnicities react to terrible sights and news. Some are grief-stricken and silent, some will fall to the ground and flop around like a fish, and some scream at the top of their lungs as if it were a contest to see who can show the most grief. I am not judging here; I am just telling the reader what I have observed over the years.

This call did not end there. I used a tool called a Halligan bar to prop up the hood of the truck. In all of the excitement—rookie!—I forgot the bar when we left the scene. This was discovered later, and it looked as if I was going to have to pay for a new bar. But my buddy saw the tow truck, from the scene earlier, parked at a gas station. We pulled over, and when the tow-truck driver saw four firemen coming to talk to him, he gave up the Halligan bar without a fuss.

As for me, lesson learned. Don't forget tools, and don't expect tow-truck drivers to be honest. He knew whose bar that was.

How Much Can Happen in a Night?

I was on the ambulance one night at 23's, and both Engine 23 and Ambulance 23 got called to an automobile that was witnessed driving off the road and into the bayou. We raced down Lawndale to the scene. Bystanders were gathered around a set of tire tracks leading directly down the grassy bank and into the water. My partner and I got there first and ran to the bank.

A lady grabbed my shirtsleeve and said, "Hurry! He is still in there!"

I removed my glasses and was taking out my wallet when I heard my captain yell, "You stand fast, rookie! You are not swift-water qualified"—at the time, I was not—"and you cannot see a thing."

A Houston bayou is not the Frio or Comal River. Those rivers are spring fed and gin clear, but the bayou is a nasty, dirty, dark-chocolate soup that, mysteriously, Houston is known to brag about. My captain was right. I could not even tell if the car was still in the same spot at which it had entered the water. Who knows what other debris was under that water, waiting to trap me? Sitting here now, drinking coffee and writing this, I laugh at my rookie thoughts back then. But I don't apologize for them. It is my instinct to want to try to do something, but sometimes nothing can be done.

The captain called the rescue truck and, upon surveying the situation, eventually called the HPD dive team. This was now a recovery, not a rescue. We waited longer than I expected for HPD to find the car, and it indeed took a while because the slow but steady current had pushed the car about thirty yards downstream from the point of entry.

The news choppers and vans arrived on scene, and the family of the man, upon seeing the news coverage and hearing the vehicle description, showed up as well. The report was that the driver had been drinking all day. They waited for the hour or so it took for HPD to state they had found the vehicle and were going to dive to retrieve the body. There were probably around eight to ten family members on the bank when the HPD diver emerged with the body and started bringing it to the shore. As soon as the body broke the surface of the water, the family let loose with screams and wails as they cried and fell to the ground. So much so that I had to go grab one of the little ones a family member was holding so she would not drop the child. It was a sad sight to see such grief.

We stayed on scene for a while; the engine went back in service before we did. We left the scene around 1:00 a.m. About thirty minutes after we went back in service, we and the engine caught a run with Medic 29 to a club at which there had been a stabbing. My fellow rookie—who happened to also be my best friend from high school and the one who actually talked me into applying to the fire department—was on the engine and later related to me the story of the victim.

A very beautiful girl was at the club, and whether this is true or not, it was reported that she was going around the club, asking guys for drinks, and then not talking to them. One guy became very upset and approached the girl from behind, reached around to her front with a small blade, and stuck her just below her breastbone. Not a deep puncture, but just enough to hit the vena cava and cause her to start bleeding out internally. The medic unit got there, grabbed my buddy off the pumper to help on the ride to the hospital, loaded the girl, and took off for Ben Taub Hospital. She later was pronounced dead in the shock room at Ben Taub.

Two fatalities so far in one night, the ambulance went back into service and returned to the station with the pumper. I decided to wait for the medic unit to bring my buddy back from the hospital. About an hour later, Medic 29 showed up and dropped him off at the station.

While talking to the paramedics on 29's about the last call, a car swerved into the station's driveway, and a guy jumped out and yelled that his friend had been shot by a shotgun. The victim was in the passenger seat, leaning over and bleeding from the torn flesh down his right side. We removed him from the vehicle and loaded him into the medic unit, and they took off for Ben Taub one more time. They had been in service, after the stabbing victim, for less than five minutes.

I remember thinking that this was one night, at one station, in this large city. I wondered how much more could happen in one night.

Man vs. Train

I had been working for a month or so when, about midnight, we were called to a vehicle-train accident over in a large train yard near the Ship Channel. A bridge has since been constructed as an overpass to this set of several tracks that citizens have to traverse to enter a neighborhood. I was on the ambulance with a good partner who had several years in, and we arrived to find a train stopped in the intersection, but no car anywhere. On the ground and around the tracks, we did observe some type of scraping and dragging marks pointing in the direction the train must have been traveling.

It was dark, so we grabbed our Wolf lights (large flashlights) and started down the tracks. About 100 yards down, we began to see cars off the tracks, train wheels and truck wheels separated from each other and scattered about. We finally arrived at the tangled, busted mess of metal that used to be a vehicle, a trail of car parts behind it, about 200 yards down from the intersection. It was upside down, the roof lying between the tracks. We instantly looked for bodies and saw legs buried in the twisted metal, but because of the amount of damage to the car, it was difficult to see the rest of the body. My partner and a couple of others were opposite me and closest to the body. So, naturally, they started to try to feel for a pulse on one of the ankles.

While they were doing that, I got on the ground and shone my light under the wreck, trying to see what I could. I started with my flashlight beam to the left and slowly worked it to the right. I yelled to the crew that they could stop checking for a pulse. When they yelled back, "Why?" I told them that I was looking at the man's vertebrae sticking out of his torso where his head should be. No head, but shoulders with white, cervical vertebrae jutting out.

We could also smell the alcohol, so we started looking around for other victims who may have been ejected from the vehicle. It was doing this that we found out what happened to the man's head. While stepping over the tracks, my foot squished in some kind of soft material. I directed my light beam towards the ground and saw I was stepping on brain matter, skin, and hair. I told the other firefighter, and together we saw where the top part of the man's head first made contact with a crosstie and each one after that. Every few crossties there was a chunk of brain matter, bone, and eventually his teeth smeared down the line of the tracks. We figured that as the car was upside down and being crushed and pushed along the tracks, first, the roof went, and then each crosstie acted like a huge cheese grater on the car and man until the train came to a halt.

We talked to a witness who stated that the car was waiting for the train to pass. He must have become tired of waiting or passed out while the car was in gear, but he drove up under the train right in between a boxcar's wheels, and the carnage began there.

One of the things I remember the most is having to get bystanders away from the brains and bones smeared along the tracks. People were letting their little kids get up close and look at what was once a human head. Not to mention that it was after midnight. Why weren't these kids in bed? Of course, I yelled at the bystanders to get back because this was a biohazard. Not only does one not know what kind of blood-borne diseases this person had, if any, but who allows their children to gaze upon such things? I still do not understand people's fascination with death and gore; this type of crowd behavior happens at every violent or gruesome scene.

Like a Horror Movie

I remember during EMT class, all those years ago, our instructors telling us that the first time we physically do CPR on a person's chest, the popping that is heard on the first few pumps will be strange. I can tell you that is true. When the sternum separates from the ribs with the first two or three compressions, there is a popping or cracking sound that is indeed strange to the rookie EMT.

I have performed CPR so many times it would be impossible to remember all of them, but I do remember a few. One was an old lady we made who presented lying in her bed as if asleep. Her home provider called us, and, of course, we started checking vital signs. No pulse and no respirations, but the body was still warm. We give everybody the best chance we can, so our protocols call for "working" the body until we either transport to the nearest ER or the patient is field terminated.

As we prepared to do bag-valve-mask (BVM) ventilation and got the oxygen out, I started chest compressions. The other guys began using the BVM, and soon my captain spotted the stomach begin to get slightly bigger. We repositioned the airway to stop air from going down the esophagus into the stomach and continued to work the patient. While all of this is going on, the home nurse is giving us her medical history, which happened to include stomach cancer.

The paramedics arrived, and CPR was halted for a few seconds to check for vital signs on the monitor. Those few seconds were all that was needed for the air that had been pushed into her stomach to start back out, carrying copious amounts of blood from the stomach cancer up and out of her mouth. She was lying there in her bed with her head on her pillow, and blood was flowing out of her mouth, down her face and chin, and onto her pillow. Not a small trickle either, I mean mouthfuls of the stuff. At first, I did not know what had happened, and my captain looked at me and just stated, "Stomach cancer." I remember thinking to myself, while looking down at this woman with her mouth open and blood oozing out, it looked like something from a horror movie. I felt very sorry for this lady but took comfort from knowing that she was not really there, as her spirit had left this body a while ago.

After repeated CPR and all cardiac protocols, and considering her age, her advanced stage of cancer, and the last time she was seen awake, attempts to revive her were halted. She was gone and not coming back, and the fact she was warm when we arrived was due more to her being under the covers than from her just having passed away. Compared to other calls, this was a very ordinary call. I just still remember the blood coming out and catching me off guard.

So This Is Christmas

On Christmas Day of my rookie year, I was to take my turn on the box (work in the ambulance). By this time, the ambulance had started to become a source of irritation due to all of the rampant abuse of the emergency system by the citizens of Houston. A source of irritation that lasted for many years to come.

Certain people must work on Christmas day. Of course, police and fire and ER staff, but it seems gas-station attendants and movie-theater staff as well. So floating on the camaraderie of knowing that society would fall to pieces if we all were not working, I set off on my day on the ambulance.

It was one of my worst days on the box. We made fifteen runs, but that is not why; at Station 9, and 28 later in my career, I made more than that every shift. I think because as a rookie, I was surprised that the nonsense people call in for does not even take a break on Christmas Day. I have worked several Christmas Days since then—it is just part of my profession as a firefighter—but this was the first time in my life to work my ass off on Christmas Day at any job.

The only call I remember from that day was an older lady who called us to check her blood pressure. My driver and I took her vitals while she was sitting on her couch. I remember that her house was clean and tidy, a rarity for this neighborhood, and she lived alone. Her vitals were fine; she felt fine and had no medical history other than "normal" blood-pressure issues.

After talking to her for a few minutes, she finally let on about why she called. She had just talked with her daughter on the phone and had become upset after an argument. It seemed her daughter had a female "life partner" and was living a lifestyle her mother thought improper. She was so angry she called 911; she just wanted someone to talk to, I suppose. I have talked to many, many people on calls over the years who just needed another person there to listen.

So, you see, the fire service is the catchall for anything from putting out fires to containing toxic spills, to fielding complaints about "my daughter who is a lesbian."

If You Don't Want to Be in Trouble, Don't Go Where Trouble Lives

Late one night, my partner and I were driving back from a call on the ambulance when we got hit with another call for an injured party. This was years before computer-aided dispatch, so further information was a rare thing, and "injured party" could mean just about anything.

The call was in another district, only a couple of miles from the medical center. We arrived to find a White male sitting on the lawn of a house; he was surrounded by seven or eight Hispanic males—not good. The kid in the middle looked as if the Mexican guys had beat him up pretty severely from all of the blood and swelling that I noticed just as we pulled up. No cops, no engine company, just Ambulance 23 on this scene.

I got out and started walking to the obvious patient, but the group closed their ranks and basically blocked my access to him. I stopped and, as calmly as I could, told them the police were on the way—they were not—and if they didn't let me help this guy, they were all going to go to jail. Needless to say, I was pretty nervous, but after a few seconds, they began to back away and let me get to the patient. He was covered in blood, and the only thing he said was that he was thirsty. Understandable, because if you have ever been in any kind of fight, thirst is one of the things you notice most.

Usually, you do a primary size-up of the patient where they are, then get the stretcher, help the patient onto the stretcher, and load the patient into the ambulance. But due to the fact that there were several angry *vatos locos* wanting to dish out more violence, I grabbed the kid and basically pulled him into the ambulance, shut the door with the thugs following us, and told my driver to take off for Ben Taub.

Once inside the box and away from the scene, I checked his radial pulse, which was rapid, but it also told me he had a systolic pressure of at least 70, so I put him on oxygen and started to address the copious bleeding from his face and head. He was spitting large amounts of blood, which could or could not make him gag, and he had lacerations and lumps all over his body, a broken nose, and swollen eyes. He also had bruises and abrasions on his torso and arms from the beating. Internal injuries and bleeding were not out of the question.

I asked him what he was doing there. As if I didn't know. He stated that the drug deal went bad; they beat him up, held a gun to his head, and forced him to call his parents to say goodbye. He was a kid—aka, dumbass—from the suburbs who went to the hood to buy some drugs, but instead he got robbed and came very close to being killed.

I was pulling out the blood-pressure cuff when he said the words you never want to hear from a patient—"I feel like I am going to die." When a patient says that, you take it seriously. We were already Code 2, but I told my driver to step on the gas pedal, and I stopped tending to his bleeding and started to take a blood pressure. My driver yelled back that we were almost there. We were pulling up to the hospital as I was trying to get a blood-pressure reading for the second time. I was having trouble hearing his pressure and was about to palpate it when we backed into the loading bay of the ER, and the doors opened. The kid was still alert and talking, but I was worried about him.

We wheeled him into Ben Taub, and I immediately put the pressure cuff on him and told the nurse we had a short transport during which I could not get an accurate pressure on him. The machine said his systolic pressure was 52, meaning he had lost a lot of blood and was what is called "hypovolemic." No wonder I could not hear his pressure during transport. When I got him into the box, he was in compensated shock. During the short ride, his body decompensated, and his blood pressure dropped.

He was rushed to the shock room, where IV fluids eventually brought his vitals back to normal. He stated he felt as if he was about to die in the ambulance because he was indeed about to die. The fact that transport to the ER only lasted a few minutes saved his life. I happened to talk to the attending doctor a few days later and learned that the kid was fine and was at home recovering.

As a rookie EMT and firefighter, this call taught me a lot. Even though in the order of patient assessment, blood pressure comes after airway, breathing, circulation, C-spine stabilization, mental status, and the rapid head-to-toe assessment of the patient, the situation will dictate the actual order of events. Sometimes, a BP, especially when in the back by yourself—as I was—needs to be first. His extreme thirst was not just from the fight, but due to his low fluid volume.

I also learned from experience, not just from what I heard in the classroom, that when a patient says they feel as if they are about to die, they know what they are talking about. Experienced medics, and even I now, look back at this and say duh, but the reader has to remember that I was a basic EMT, a rookie with maybe three months' experience at that time and by myself in the back of a BLS (basic life support) ambulance, trying to take care of this guy. In other words, I had no ability to start an IV and give him fluids. I thank the Lord that we had a very short transport time.

Kicking Field Goals

Homeless people and the typical "street person" make up a large part of your call volume, depending on which station you are working and in what part of the city that station is located. Obviously, stations near downtown, where most homeless shelters are located, have a higher concentration of homeless calls, but almost all stations deal with street people at one time or another. Station 23 was no different.

One run that sticks out in my mind was a call that both Medic 29 and Ambulance 23 made together for chest pain. As usual, because the medic unit usually waits for a "disregard," we arrived first and found a homeless guy sitting near a fence about ten yards or so from the street, the strong smell of alcohol upon him. He was immediately rude and not very cooperative. Since he claimed he had chest pain, we could not disregard the medic unit, and they arrived a few minutes after us.

The usual crew was on Medic 29 that day, and when the paramedic did not get his beloved disregard and then heard the guy would not let us take vitals, he lost some of his patience with the guy. The paramedic started asking the man why he called if he did not want us to touch him. Well, this made the guy mad, and he started dropping f-bombs on the paramedic and saying things about effing firemen, and such and so forth. Well, in turn, this made the medic even more pissed off, which pissed off the drunk even more and made him even more agitated at us. The driver on Medic 29 called for PD to respond to our location. Understand, this is coming from a homeless guy who dialed 911 and is now cussing us out.

We informed the man that PD was on the way, and more cuss words and irritation flew our way. He was sitting on his butt with his shoes off the entire time, but when he heard PD was coming, he started to grab one shoe and put it on. The angle he held the shoe with—holding the toe area with his fingers, the heel resting on the ground—looked exactly as you would holding the football as a kid when your buddy wanted to kick it to start a neighborhood game. Not wanting the man to get away, I guess, the medic saw too ripe an opportunity when the way the guy was putting on his shoe formed the perfect imitation of a placeholder holding the ball for a field goal. The medic took a step forward, brought his right leg back, and in perfect NFL form, kicked the bum's shoe up in the air about twenty feet and about twenty feet away. I could not believe my eyes; it was perfect and so funny I cheered. Of course, f-bombs galore came out of the caller's mouth as he went to retrieve his shoe. We informed him that he was not going anywhere before the cops could get there.

Not having learned his lesson the first time, I guess, the caller got back in the same position and tried to put his shoe on the exact same way. Well, the medic backed up again, lined up the shoe, and kicked another "field goal" just as pretty as the first one. The drunk got up to get his shoe again just as the cops rolled up, and, lo and behold, the homeless guy became so polite and nice when PD was on the scene. Of course, we asked him why he was so nice now and was so rude earlier.

He was arrested for being drunk and taken away. I often wonder if that medic, who is a captain today, remembers doing his best Jankowski impression with a drunk home-less person's shoe.

The Hispanic Panic

This next story has played out in one form or another many, many times in my career, but before becoming a fire-fighter, I had never heard of it. The Hispanic panic is a very common call. **I did not make up the name**; I am simply telling the reader what it is known by on the streets. This must be a statewide reference because I have friends in the San Antonio FD, Austin FD, and New Braunfels FD who refer to it by the same name. And yes, even the Hispanic guys use the name because that is just what it is called in the fire service. Once again, this term is not my creation.

The behavior is most commonly associated with non-English-speaking Hispanic women, although I am sure each culture has its own variation. The usual routine goes something akin to this: the husband comes home from either a hard day at work or a hard night drinking, and he and his wife get into an argument. Sometimes this leads to the husband striking the woman, but most of the time not. The woman will hyperventilate on purpose and put on a very convincing show of being in a state of respiratory distress or chest discomfort, therefore making the man feel guilty and usually resulting in a call to 911. Many times, it will be a mother or grandmother who gets into an argu-ment with kids or grandkids, and the same routine plays out. After taking vitals, the first question is always, "Was she fighting with someone?"

One call that was a true learning experience for me as a rookie was to an apartment late one night for "difficulty breathing." True to form, no one spoke any English in the house. I speak passable *español*—enough to pass the city's bilingual exam and receive bilingual pay—so I usually can pick up on the main points. Also true to form, the man had come home after the bar closed and had started a fight with his wife; she followed the game plan to perfection.

When we arrived, I found a woman on the floor; she appeared to be "guppy breathing" and had an ashen appearance. She truly appeared to be in respiratory distress and would not answer any questions. I asked my driver to call for a medic unit and started the woman on oxygen. When Medic 40 arrived, the woman, who had calmed down some, started the labored breathing all over again. Now I knew I had been had; I had called the medic at 2:00 a.m. for nothing. The driver on Medic 40 was Hispanic and spoke Spanish fluently; he immediately told the woman that if she did not behave and act normally, he and his partner were going to be forced to put a plastic tube down her throat (intubate her). She continued her act, the medic repeated his message, and they began to open their bags and act as though it were about to happen. This got her attention, and she almost immediately calmed down and returned to normal behavior.

After checking vitals and the medic unit getting a signed refusal for transport, we all started back to our units. I felt stupid and apologized to the paramedics for calling them out on what eventually became a "no load" (non-transport). I simply admitted that I could not tell she was faking; she had fooled me, and it probably sounded dumb to dispatch for me to request a medic unit, only to have the call result in a signed refusal.

The medic was a good guy; he just laughed and said not to worry about it. He got called to a cardiac arrest one time with CPR in progress, only to arrive and find a guy lying down on the street and yelling, "Ow...ow...ow...ow," every time the man above him did a chest compression.

Overall General Impression

I have only written down a fraction of the runs I made while stationed at 23's. Most runs are the same old abdominal pains, headaches, or the ever-popular "unknown problem," which can be anything. But the Houston Ship Channel has its own identity. It is solidly Hispanic, and the area of Harrisburg, which is around where Buffalo Bayou enters the Ship Channel, is actually older than the city of Houston. I have seen old frontier maps of Texas; Harrisburg is shown, but Houston is not. So, having worked in several totally different parts of Houston, I can offer a general impression of each.

Besides a hardworking, blue-collar population, there was one thing the Harrisburg area seemed to have in abundance, and that was youth trying to be "hard" and prove something to somebody. The wannabe gangsters, with their "Hu-stone" (Houston) tattoos, were at almost every call. Many times, I was called to clean up the face of one of these types who had been fighting with the cops and, according to the police, "fallen down." Some of them helped out on scene by translating, and some of them acted as if they wanted to fight you when you walked in the door, even though they were the ones who had called you for assistance. Of course, they think they are tough and are so "bad to the bone" because that is the culture in which they grow up, I guess. It almost seems a male rite of passage to follow this pattern, and after seeing them at almost every run, they just become part of the hood cliché.

Station 23 was my introduction to the fire service and all of the things that come along with this career. Station life is part of that, and the normal rookie tasks of memorizing territory and being checked out on critical skills with the truck and hoses were all part of the process. Jokes were played daily, as was basketball.

I met several characters. One was the guy every rookie heard about in the academy—he ate a dead guy's hamburger on scene. The story goes that as the victim came out of a burger joint, a car jumped a curb and pinned him to a telephone pole, killing him instantly. The dead guy was still clutching his burger bag. This fireman got out his trauma shears, cut open the bag, and ate his hamburger while waiting for the coroner. When I met him, he was nice…but as strange as you think it takes to do a thing like that, to say the least.

Fish were put under the hoods of private citizens' trucks, only to start stinking from the engine block's heat. Sandwiches had ingredients switched, flour was sprinkled in guys' beds, and, of course, guys were sprayed down with water. A firehouse can be like a big junior-high party at times.

It was also my first experience with sleeping in the same room with women other than my wife. The EMT room at Station 23 is small and has two beds. When on the ambulance, you sleep in the EMT room so you do not disturb the other guys when coming back in from runs all night. I slept in there every time I was on the box, except when I had a female partner. One in particular would fill in from another station and drive the ambulance; she was very attractive. I heard she still is today. Being a married man, I simply did not feel comfortable sleeping in that small room with her, so on those days, I went to sleep in the dorm with the guys. Of course, the guys made fun of me for it, but to me, it was the only choice.

Then there is cake and ice cream. Anytime you do anything for the first time, you owe cake and ice cream. Fat firemen try to milk this as much as possible, and the rookie has to eventually catch on to this and say no. But for your first fire, you better bring cake and ice cream the next day.

My first fire was a pretty large machine-shop fire, and to my relief, I did well. All rookies are nervous about this huge step, but I pulled the line, went in with the nozzle, and "put the wet stuff on the red stuff" without any hesitation. We "put a good stop" on the fire, and my captain was pleased. The thing I remember most about my first "real" burner was not the fire itself, but how we firemen noticed it.

We were grocery shopping, and I had just stated that not only would I bring cake and ice cream for my first fire, I would also buy dinner. Well, while walking out to the pumper from the store, lo and behold, there was a column of black smoke in the distance, in the direction of the station. Only one thing looks like that, and every fireman knows it—structure fire. As we jumped into the pumper, and the call started to come in over the radio, I remember our driver saying something about "Joel buying dinner" the next day on shift. Of all the luck.

And, oh yeah, rats—lots of rats—always ran out of the houses when they were on fire. While "on the nozzle," I have seen dozens bunched up under eaves on the roof and coming out of the doors and windows, jumping to the ground. One house fire had so many rats on the roof that it completely distracted me from what I was doing for a few seconds.

Chapter 2

Station 34

About six months into my career, the city balanced its staffing levels at stations across the entire department and moved probationary rookies anywhere there was a need. I was sent from Station 23 to Station 34 on the northeast side of the city. Leaving my station and friends was not fun, but the worst part for me was the fact that I had been memorizing my territory at 23's and had it down pretty well at that time. Now—*boom!*—an entirely new territory to start studying.

But in the long run, my time at 34's was a good thing for my career. I made many more fires than at 23's; the EMS calls were usually more violent as well. I worked with some guys for whom, to this day, I have a great deal of respect; they helped me finish my probationary year strong.

Russian Roulette

I will never ever forget a call on Engine 34 to a house full of panic. The call came in as a GSW (gunshot wound), and that is a call in which firemen wait for the police to declare the scene threat-free before you enter to treat the patient. That whole thing about firemen not having guns and not wearing bulletproof vests is the reason the cops go in first.

PD declared the scene safe before we arrived, and upon arrival, we were directed to the back room of the house. I happened to be the first one in the room and saw a young Hispanic male with a closely cropped haircut lying on his face in a pool of blood. His cousin was in the corner, yelling in disbelief, and a .38 revolver was just a few inches from the dead teenager's hand (which I thought was odd, by the way—PD usually removes any guns from the scene right away). On the very back of the teen's head was a hole with chunks of bone and brain in and around it. DRT, or "dead right there," in unofficial fireman talk.

I asked what happened, and the cousin in the corner stated that the gun fired while they were playing Russian roulette. I turned, looked at him, and simply asked, "What?" He simply repeated what he said and was led out of the room by the police who also took the revolver as evidence. I looked at the other guys, and they just shrugged their shoulders. Somebody commented that maybe they were high or thought the gun was unloaded, but to me, Russian roulette was an urban legend. A myth that maybe was true about Russian gulag guards who made prisoners do this for entertainment, not something American teenagers actually participated in. We checked vitals without moving the body as best we could, and as it looked, there was nothing but a flat line on the monitor. The kid was sixteen.

We went out to the front yard to put our gear back on the trucks and were sort of talking about the call. An elderly Hispanic lady walked right up to me. Her face said it all; she was the mother. She asked me in Spanish, "*¿Mijo muerto?*" ("Is my son dead?")

I answered in surprise, "*Lo siento, pero sí, está muerto.*" ("I'm sorry, but yes, he is dead.")

She nodded her head in understanding, turned around, and walked back into the house. It was almost as if this was an outcome she had been expecting for years. There was pain in her eyes but also acceptance.

I looked at my partners and told them that she either just now learned her son was dead, or she just wanted to hear the final word from the fireman who examined him. "*¿Quién sabe?*"

Fries with That?

On about my second or third week at 34's, we made a GSW east of the station at a fast-food joint a mile or two down on Laura Koppe Drive. The cops were on the scene before we got there, proving yet again that they could beat us in when they wanted to. A car was on the median and still pretty much in a straight line from the drive-through window of the fast-food joint.

We jumped out to investigate and found a female sitting in the driver's seat with her eyes open; her right hand was still holding the "to-go" box of whatever food she ordered. She almost looked alive and normal, except for the three bullet holes in her chest.

Witnesses said that she had just paid for and received her order when her ex-husband showed up in front of her car, pulled a gun, and blasted away, killing her right there in the car. Her foot must have come off the brake and her car, at idle speed, left the window and stayed straight across the two lanes until the curb stopped the rear wheel from going all the way up on the grass median. I remember thinking that 34's district sure was in a different part of town from the Ship Channel.

Like a Glove

I was standing on the back patio of Station 34, talking with another firefighter while he was smoking a cigarette. He spotted the faint bit of smoke first and commented on it. About ten seconds later, the smoke was thick enough to conclude that something was on fire coming from the southwest, around Jenson Drive. We ran inside and announced that we had a burner. Everyone jumped up and got on the trucks, and the smoke was thick and black enough by then to aim the trucks in the general direction.

Before we got down the block, the call came over dispatch—a car fire with possible fatalities on the Hardy Toll Road. I have made so many car fires in my career that they really became more of a nuisance than anything. You have to pull a line most times, always be fully bunked up, and many times wait forever for arson to arrive on scene before you can leave after the few minutes it takes to put out a car fire.

When you are one of the firefighters in the back, "bunking up" (putting on your bunker gear, which means firefighting gear) as the truck is going to the call, you are concentrating on getting your gear on properly, and the next thing you know sometimes is you are at the scene. I was riding FF—first line (tasked with deploying the first attack line, or hose, off the pumper, as opposed to those riding plugs, whose job is to catch the fire hydrant). So I jumped off and grabbed the nozzle of the attack line.

This car was fully involved by the time we arrived, and that means there was not just an engine fire; the entire front, middle, and trunk were "blowing and going." Two passengers were standing away from the car, and the captain told me a third, who never made it out of the vehicle, was still in the back seat. I don't know how that happens. Maybe he was very drunk, but I never heard.

We hit the interior section first and put the car fire out from there. Car fires, no matter how fully involved, usually don't take too long to extinguish. You could see the poor guy sitting in the back seat, burned to a crisp. It looked unreal, like a charred-black mannequin, and I just felt sorry for the guy. I turned around to pull the hose back while the rest of the crew and paramedics rushed to the victim. To my surprise, they loaded him on the stretcher. He still had a pulse somehow, some way. He later died, as was expected, but you give everybody a fighting chance.

I took my gear off, except for my bunker pants, as did my partner, and we started the process of waiting for arson while picking up our gear and tools. I was washing down the scene when I saw a leather glove floating on the water towards the drain. I put the hose down to retrieve it and keep someone from buying a new pair of overhaul gloves. I bent down to pick it up but paused because it just looked strange. I studied it for a few more seconds and then realized what I was looking at—the burned guy's outer layer of skin from his wrist to his fingers had been shed somehow; it had come off his body in the almost-perfect form of a hand. It was stiff, hardened, and hollow, and it looked as though a person could almost insert their hand as if putting on a glove. I showed a few of the guys, and all agreed that was the first time we had seen something like that.

Castor Oil Fixes It

When there is a need across the district, firemen take turns doing what is called "filling in." When you fill in, you go to another firehouse that is low on manpower, and you work your twenty-four-hour shift there. Usually, no one likes to fill in because you have to pack up everything—including your gear, bedding, and locker stuff—that you will use during the twenty-four hours. But filling in is just part of the job; when you are promoted to engineer, it usually comes to a stop.

One shift, I went to fill in at Station 43 in a neighborhood called Settegast. It is a traditionally Black neighborhood going up Wayside Drive, north of the Fifth Ward, which is probably the most well-known Black community in Houston. Station 43 is a busy station that makes fires regularly, but mainly you go on EMS calls throughout the day and night.

On the pumper, we made a seizure call to a local corner store, and when we arrived, we found a crowd of twenty or more people surrounding a man lying down on his back in the parking lot. We made our way through the crowd to the man and found another man kneeling over him and pouring a small bottle down the victim's throat. The first rule of seizure calls—and all calls, for that matter—is to maintain a clear airway, so I immediately asked the man just what in the heck he was doing.

"Castah oil fixes seiz-ures," he replied.

We immediately took the bottle out of the victim's mouth and checked his vitals. It was then we noticed two other empty bottles lying beside the man's head. "Did you pour these bottles down his throat too?" I asked, to which he replied yes and repeated what he said about castor oil being the cure-all for seizures.

The engineer on the pumper that day was an old country boy from East Texas. Upon sizing up that the man had about twenty-four ounces of castor oil in his belly, he stated, "Well, one thing is for sure—he is gonna be up shitting all night long."

Like a Dog

Near the intersection of Laura Koppe Road and Jensen Drive there was a multistory assisted-living complex, or "old folks' home" in the local jargon. It may still be there; I am not sure. But if it is not, I am not surprised that it closed down. We hated making runs to this place. We all felt sorry for the people who were forced to live there and for all the elderly who were forced to live in any low-budget nursing home, but this place was one of our least favorite. (Later on in my career, I remember being so thankful that before my grandfather died, he had enough money to afford a decent nursing home.) Many, many times we went to this location for anything from CPR to a simple assist call. One call in particular angered me so much that I literally wanted to punch someone on the staff.

We were dispatched for another "assist the citizen" call to this location. We arrived, went up the elevator to the room, and found an elderly lady lying on the floor on her right side, a tray of food about an inch from her face. She was trying to somehow scrape food from the lunch tray into her mouth with her left hand because she was lying on her right arm. She was not propped up in any way with a pillow or anything.

Of course, we asked what happened. We were told that the old lady fell while trying to walk across the floor and could not get back up. I asked why the staff had not helped her up. The reply we received from one of the staff members was that when they had helped up a previous patient, that person was injured, the company was sued, and the facility had to pay damages. So, now, the staff was required to call 911 for lifting assistance and just leave the tenant on the floor until we arrived to pick them up. (I am not making this up.) I then asked why her lunch was on the floor. We were told that lunch trays were being passed out, and since she was on the floor, they just put the tray on the floor next to her so she could get to it.

A righteous anger arose in me, and I looked at my captain, who was clearly angered also. My captain asked in a very agitated voice, "So y'all just feed her on the floor like a dog?"

No answer. Good thing, because no answer would have been correct. More out of pure sympathy than out of duty, we picked this poor lady up, put her in bed, and checked her vitals. We then picked up her lunch tray and set it in front of her so she could eat with dignity like a human being.

Guns Ablazing

One of the more strange calls I went on happened when I was stationed at 34's but had to fill in at Station 6. Around noon, we got a fire call with smoke showing and police on scene, so I ran to the pumper and started to bunk up. The captain at 6's at that time was a notoriously hard-assed captain, and I wanted to make a good impression on him for no other reason than to keep him off my back.

We made the scene, and indeed light smoke was visible. There was also a bleeding guy handcuffed on the sidewalk right in front of the front door. I jumped off and grabbed the nozzle, and we had to literally step over the yelling, bleeding guy lying in our way to make entry. The guys on the ambulance started to tend to him while we "got our water" and went into the house.

The house was large, and the smoke was light, so visibility was still pretty good. With general ease, we were able to advance the hose to the seat of the fire and put water on the burning material, which was a large roll of sheet paper, the kind that big printing shops use. It was then we started to notice a mattress with a camera on a tripod in almost every corner of the house. We went into a back bedroom to check for fire, and there were about a dozen TVs and computer equipment on a table in front of a chair. He was probably running some kind of home-made porn shop out of his house, and it was very creepy, to say the least.

Just then, the captain got a call over the radio for us to get out immediately. We dropped the line (when an emergency-evacuation order is given, pulling the hose line out will take too much time) and followed it out to the pumper, where we were told to stand fast. There was information that indicated the house was booby-trapped somehow.

It was then we learned what happened. The guy was behind on his rent and had been on the phone with the landlord. It turned into an argument, and the renter stated that he would just burn the place down and then hung up on the landlord. So, of course, the landlord called the cops and told them what was happening. When the cops arrived, he had already set the paper roll on fire and decided to meet the police with guns blazing. HPD saw smoke coming out from the house, called HFD, and a few minutes before we arrived, had a shoot-out with the guy as he ran out of the front door while firing at the cops. We pulled up very shortly after and advanced the hose while stepping over this idiot.

We waited for about an hour while the HPD bomb squad cleared the building, and then we went in to check things out again. The fire was long since put out, and the smoke was gone. Indeed, this guy had cameras wired from each room to the back bedroom where all the TVs were. It was a strange call, and I was glad when they cut us from the scene.

I Don't Blame the Father

While returning from yet another transport on Ambulance 32, we caught a run about halfway back to the station—an MVA (motor-vehicle accident) at the intersection of Highway 59 and Crosstimbers. We arrived on scene to see Engine 34, Ladder 34, and a couple of medic units working on a demolished car with the extrication tools. Debris was everywhere, and there was an eighteen-wheeler with a large amount of damage about fifty feet away, nearer to the intersection.

As soon as we stopped, a patient was presented to us to be "packaged" and transported. While taking care of this, I asked what happened and was told the big truck plowed over the car containing three teenage girls, and one was DOA (dead on arrival); they were working on getting the other girl out.

Before we could get the patient ready to go, a man wanting to know what happened showed up on the scene.

When he saw his dead daughter in the wreckage and his other daughter being worked on, he made a beeline to the truck driver and attacked him viciously. I remember it took three cops to hold him back and keep him on the ground. As I got into the back of the box, I remember thinking that I didn't blame the father at all; something like that would probably send me into a state of temporary insanity.

I remember when my oldest son suffered a leg fracture when a large rock flake fell off while we were bouldering (a type of rock climbing). After bandaging the wound, carrying him to the trailhead, and getting him into the ambulance, I followed the box to the hospital. On that ride, I was angry—very angry—that my son was hurt, and I wanted to punch anything or anybody. A very primal reaction, for sure, but I was that angry over my son being hurt. I do not want to imagine what that man felt seeing his daughter dead in a destroyed car that day.

The patient we transported was conscious and talking all the way to the hospital, which is a good thing. About three minutes out from the ER, I had taken my vital signs, addressed the most serious bleeding, and was doing a head-to-toe survey of her injuries when she started saying through the oxygen mask that she was "not feeling good." Any EMT will tell you this is a bad thing—remember, I was a basic EMT.

I restarted my vitals and survey. She was a teenage girl and had many thick, braided weaves attached to her scalp.

I was cursing the weaves under my breath as I tried to examine her head and was thinking about pulling some of her weaves apart and trying to cut them in order to find out what was going on. That is when we stopped, and the reverse beeps started, indicating we were backing up to Ben Taub's loading dock. We wheeled her out, and she went straight to the shock room's ever-ready, eager doctors.

It took a while to clean the ambulance of all of the blood and complete my record. Before we left the hospital, I went to check on my patient. One of the doctors in the shock room told me she had suffered internal trauma and was in serious condition but doing okay. She also had head injuries; her hair braids had been pushed into the wounds by the trauma and were actually clogging up the wound, reducing the amount of bleeding that usually is associated with scalp injuries. I was grateful then that I did not pull the braids out, which could have started an entirely new level of bleeding in the back of the box. It reminded me of how they used cobwebs in the Civil War to bandage wounds and control bleeding.

The Only English He Knows?

The engine and Medic 34 made a GSW one night at an apartment complex; we arrived to find a Hispanic male lying on the ground and in pain. The usual crowd was gathered, and the police were talking to people when we walked up to examine the patient. That day, I was the only crew member who spoke Spanish, so I went to work asking what happened and where he was hurt. He told me that he was shot in the ankle and had no other injuries. We did a full head-to-toe exam to see if there were any other wounds, and then my buddy proceeded to cut his shoe off the hurt foot and remove the sock to examine the wound.

Once the sock came off, a flood of foot odor reached his nose, and my partner calmly requested that I ask the man if he had ever heard of "fast actin' Tinactin." We chuckled a little as we found three small bullet holes in the man's ankle and foot.

The man moaned, "¡AY! ¡AY! ¡AY!" over and over while we cleaned the wounds.

The HPD officer came up to the back of the box and told me to ask the man who shot him. So I did in Spanish.

He stopped moaning, looked up, and yelled in English, "Threeee neeeegers!." No joke, nothing added by the writer here; that is **exactly** what he said.

Not believing what I heard, I asked in Spanish if he said three Black guys shot him. This time, he responded simply with a *sí*.

I looked at the cop, who happened to be Black. The cop had looked up from his clipboard upon hearing the patient's first answer. The officer shook his head and asked, "Did he say what I thought he said?"

I simply answered yes.

He then said, "So he doesn't speak any English but knows how to say that?!?" as he continued shaking his head and writing the report.

Don't Disturb His Spirit

We made a call one time to a cardiac arrest in the Kashmere Gardens area and arrived on scene to find a home full of people. There were probably ten to twelve people in the living room, sitting around, and a few on the couch, playing video games.

I knocked and walked in with the AED (automatic external defibrillator) ready, but nobody paid us any attention. Mind you, this was a cardiac-arrest call, and time was of the essence. I asked if someone called 911, and after a few seconds, someone finally took his hand off the game controller and pointed down the hallway without saying a word.

We responders went down the hall to a crowded bedroom in which a man was lying in bed, under covers. No pulse, no breathing—CPR time. As we started to get the stuff out and asked people to leave the room, we were met with objections.

"Don't do that. You will disturb his spirit," one lady said.

The patient was still warm, and HFD "works" all patients who have not assumed room temperature yet. For all we know, these people wanted the man dead for some reason. The protest became louder, and we asked if there were any DNR (do not resuscitate) papers. Someone answered yes, but of course did not know where they were.

DNR papers are supposed to be present with the patient. After more arguing and going back and forth about not disturbing his spirit with CPR, our supervisor finally got his hands on the DNR orders, and we stopped doing our job. We packed our stuff and proceeded to leave the home while dirty looks were being thrown at us by many in the house.

We finally got the story about the man. He had cancer and passed away. The family called 911 about thirty minutes later. We responded as we should, ready to give the man every chance possible. The kicker in this story is the fact that the family assumed we would know that CPR "disturbs the spirit." I had never heard that before, and this was just another belief or custom that doesn't cross cultural lines. But if you do not want the fire department to work a patient, then do not call 911. It is that simple.

My Worst Call

After all these years and all the different calls I have been on, the one that hit me the hardest happened just after I passed my rookie probation year at 34's. I have made calls that were just as tragic, bloodier, and more chaotic (in fact, there was no blood), and in which more people died, but this call hit me hard. I believe it was because the victim was a four-year-old boy, and my son was four at the time. The victim even had the same little flattop haircut. The little boy's eyes stayed open, and he stared at me the entire time I worked on him.

I have been putting off writing this story because it still bothers me to think about it, but even the unpleasant past is as much a part of history as the good times, so avoiding it benefits no one. When I finally sat down to write this story, it actually took me a few days to finish it. Much to my surprise, the raw emotion of the call returned all these years later.

Honestly, I don't even remember how the call came in to the station. Something about a child choking, I think. I do remember I was on my debit day because the medics on M34 were both fellow Aggies and solid dudes. I also remember the senior captain, who was not there on the scene, saying something to me afterward that put him on my "absolute jerk" list to this day.

We arrived on scene to find a small boy lying on the floor of his bedroom with his eyes wide open. No pulse, no breathing, and the mother sitting across the room in a state of panic. I started CPR while the medics began getting all of their gear out in order to work the patient. The supervisor was called, and as I did chest compressions on this little guy, I prayed under my breath. Not loud. A whisper, really. But besides all of our medical interventions, prayers were all I could fall back on, I guess.

The medic heard me and asked, "Are you praying?" as he was searching for a vein to put a line in. I answered yes, and he simply said, "Good man."

An unshockable heart rhythm was found by the monitor, so we kept doing CPR and pushing cardiac drugs into this little guy. As I said, his eyes were open, and every time I looked down, I looked right back up. My son Connor was four at the time, and any EMT who is a father will tell you that tragic calls on the little guys are tough to take. Any fireman who says different is either a psychopath or lying.

As we were working on the little boy and getting him ready to transport, the mother, seeing her son having all of this work being done, flipped out; we had to call another unit to respond and take care of her.

We finally got the story of what happened. The boy was jumping on the bed and having fun, the windows were open in the room, and they had burglar bars on them. Somehow, the little guy jumped forward too far off the bed and became stuck with his little head between the burglar bars of the window. His body weight pulled him down, and he was hanging there with his head between the bars when the mother found him after an unknown amount of time. An accidental hanging on burglar bars from jumping on the bed...there seemed no limit to this world's cruelty at that moment.

We loaded him up, and I found out later that his pulses returned. The child lived for a few days but was brain-dead and later passed away. I don't even know if it is true that they got his pulses back; that is just what I heard. If ever I meet up with the medic again, I will find out what he remembers about it.

I can honestly tell you that for two hours after the call, I was numb and silent. I could still function and do my job, but I was just processing my private thoughts about that call in my own way. I teared up when I thought about those little eyes, and I knew that this call simply hit too close to home. In short, I was hurting inside. (A sadness is coming over me right now as I type this, and it has been thirteen or more years since then.) I was not the only one; everyone who worked on the kid was bothered to the core. Looking back, we should have had a CISM (critical-incident stress management) session or at least a debriefing meeting in which to talk about it.

The senior captain, who did not make the call, must have heard we were taking it hard, and he asked me if I was all right. I kind of mumbled a "yes, sir" to him, but I suppose he could see in my eyes that I was hurting really badly inside. It was hard to hide. This senior captain, the "tough fireman," then very coldly lectured me about how I better get used to it, how I needed to get tough, or I should go find another job. No encouragement, no understanding or advice on what he does when calls with children bother him. Just false bravado to sound like a tough guy. One could not find a poorer example of leadership in this situation.

Wow, what a great guy. This was coming from a captain who would double up on his bunker liners so he could "take more heat" and go deeper into fires without feeling the same amount of heat that his rookies felt, just so he could claim that the heat did not bother him.

Thanks, Captain Obvious, I knew it was part of the job; it was far from my first dead body. I knew I would see many, many more, and I have. As I said before, I have made more tragic scenes (for example, five small children drowning in the same car) with far more blood and body parts lying around (construction-crane collapse). This call just hit really close to home for me. So instead of encouraging and uplifting a young guy just starting his career, this captain comes in and berates him for—*gasp!*—a call bothering him. Very poor leadership. It tainted my view of him for years.

I know some "awesome, super" firefighters (sarcasm intended) who will read this and assume a false bravado; they will say that I am some kind of wimp or something like that. To them, I respond, "Say what you want, for the truth rests nowhere in your opinion. Every honest fireman remembers a few calls that still bother them. I did not quit the fire service. I did not stop doing my duty on the scene. I was simply a father who felt deeply the sadness of this mother over the death of her child.

Years later, I was in an incident-command class for a week, and the instructor just happened to be the same captain from all those years ago. I heard he had not changed much, but that may or may not be true. In the fire service, reputations and impressions from past events can linger for years, whether fair, true, or neither. Holding a grudge may be an Olympic-level sport for some men, but I'm not one of them; all anger does is keep you captive by that person. Besides, the Bible teaches that in order to be forgiven, one must forgive, so I let go of his remarks all those years ago and just tried to learn what I could from the class.

Station 32

The first time I was sent to 32's to fill in, we were all at the breakfast table, and a female member of their crew asked the captain if he thought I could beat her at arm wrestling. I looked at her and just laughed, which seemed to upset her, so I guessed she was serious. It seemed that she was a college athlete of some sort at one time, and she often challenged men to arm wrestle. I had heard she even beat a couple of other guys in the station. This behavior seems to indicate low self-confidence, but that is another topic. I suppose since she was probably around six feet tall and had more muscle than the average woman, combined with the fact that she had some past victories, she felt confident enough to challenge other firefighters.

Now, I am not a small man. I am not huge, by any means, but at this point in my life, I was bench-pressing right at 300 and trying to join the 1,000 Club (bench-press, squat, and deadlift a combined 1,000 pounds). I just chuckled and said, "Sure, anytime."

About an hour later, I was in the watch office; the captain came in and said that I should not arm wrestle her because she was strong. He also said that there was nothing to gain for me and everything to lose.

I looked at him, shook my head, and simply said, "Captain, you can't be serious. I promise; she will not beat me."

He said okay, got on the house speaker, and announced an arm-wrestling match in the kitchen, which brought everyone in the station to the kitchen to watch.

We sat down at the table. I was still laughing and not taking her seriously, which seemed to make her even more determined. (I am laughing right now thinking about it.) We locked hands, and the contest commenced. It lasted two to three seconds at most. I'm sure, for a female, she was strong. But, for me, it was akin to arm wrestling your thirteen-year-old little brother—no contest. Still giggling about the entire thing, I smashed her hand on the table. A cheer went up from the crowd, and I calmly stood up, looked at her, said, "Did you REALLY think you could beat me? I'm a man," and walked away.

"He's Not Going In"

Another time, I was sent to fill in at Station 32. Before I left 34's, one of the older guys pulled me aside and said, "If you make a burner with that captain that is over there today, he's not going in."

I asked, "What do you mean? How can you simply refuse to go fight fire?"

I was told by the others listening that the captain only had about four months left in the department, and he had made it clear that he was not going inside any more house fires. I said okay, got my gear, and headed out to Station 32.

Well, as luck would have it, the fire tones hit the station, and the dispatcher announced a house fire with multiple calls. When there are multiple calls to 911 for a fire, you know you are heading to a working fire.

We pulled out, onto the front slab, and to our left, about a mile away, was a huge, steady black column of smoke. The driver yelled something about "We got one!" and we headed to the fire.

The fire was in the neighborhood just down the road from the station; we parked and saw flames coming out from the back-left part of a home and heavy black smoke pouring out. I was riding first line that day, so I did my job and immediately started to pull and stretch the handline to the front door. The E/O (engineer/operator) gave us water, and as I bled the nozzle of air at the open front door, I felt a hand on my shoulder and heard a voice behind me say, "Let's go!"

So we entered the house as black smoke was starting to bank down about two feet from the ceiling. We turned left down a hallway and proceeded to make our way to the very last bedroom on the right, which had flames starting to lick out of the room through the cracked door. I opened the door to the bedroom, and the entire room was on fire. I simply opened my nozzle to a slightly larger fog pattern and proceeded to put the fire out rather quickly—standard room and contents fire.

After the fire was knocked down, we continued to wet the room down, knock out the rest of the window so ventilation could improve, and hit some hot spots. We then backed out of the house to let the house ventilate before we went back inside to pull off Sheetrock and check for fire spread.

It was when I got outside that I noticed that the voice behind me came from the other firefighter in the back and not from the captain who was standing, without any bunker gear on, and talking to the other engine companies that had arrived. It was then I remembered what was said to me earlier that morning about him. And I can attest that, indeed, we caught a house fire, and he did not go in.

Leaving 34's

Overall, I would say that I enjoyed my time at Station 34. I made many fires and got a lot of experience on many different types of EMS runs as well, but at the time, I lived in Clear Lake and wanted a shorter commute into the station than the time it took to go from basically League City to North Houston.

I remember riding next to my buddy while checking plugs (testing fire hydrants) on E34 and hearing our captain look at big houses and comment about how one would make a "good burner" that would be fun to fight. My buddy and I just looked at each other and shook our heads.

I clearly remember going into houses that we called "picket fences"—just to be in a fire, I guess. A "picket fence" is a house that has burned down to the studs but is still on fire, so it looks like a picket fence on fire. This usually only happened with the older wooden homes in the area.

We had water fights almost daily at 34's. These were the days before everyone carried expensive cell phones on them and rookies, especially rookies, "got wet" daily. It would range from simple things—such as calling the rookie around the corner of the station, and the guys with a fire hose, waiting in ambush—all the way to elaborate plans in which guys hid an IV bag in the ceiling over the rookie's bed and had it drip just enough for them to wake up with a big wet spot on their covers. One guy's favorite trick was to use a very light fishing line and a small hook to gradually pull your covers off you during the night.

I remember mopping up spot fires at a home one time, and my captain ordered me to go in and wet down the paramedics inside the house. I looked at him, and he said it was an order, so I did it. HFD paramedics never got to fight much fire, so they asked the captain if they could "go in." I guess he just wanted to mess with them. I came around the door with an open nozzle and almost knocked them down. Well, one of the medics was not going to take that lightly, so he made plans to get me back.

When we got back to the station, my driver told me to get out and "back him in" (guide him into the station in reverse). I got out, and while I was directing him back, a huge wave of water hit me from above and nearly knocked me to my knees. The medic was on top of the firehouse, and he dumped a five-gallon mop bucket of water on me.

Well, I knew the only way for him to get up there was the ladder in the access closet, so I ran to the house line, charged the line with water, and beat him to the closet. As he was about on step three of ten coming down the ladder, I opened the hose up on him for the second time that day. He started screaming curse words at me like a scalded rat. I laughed and then ran off and avoided him for a little while because I knew he would be sore at being outflanked. Years later, I relieved him on the captain's seat one morning, and we talked and laughed for an hour about 34's.

In the Hill Country, where I live now, mesquite is the BBQ wood of choice, along with oak. In East Texas, where I grew up, and in Houston, pecan wood is the wood of choice. For a man who prides himself on his BBQ, finding a surprise source of pecan wood is akin to finding a treasure trove. At 34's, there was such a man. He had a loud voice you could hear all the way across the fireground with ease; it was usually laced with a few choice curse words.

After a mild hurricane, we surveyed our "still alarm" (territory closest to the fire station that E34 responds to first and many times alone). About two blocks behind 34's, a huge pecan tree in the front yard of a home had fallen and crushed the fence. He was riding captain that day, saw the tree, and stated that he was going to get that tree the next day.

Sure enough, at shift change, he went home and hitched his flatbed trailer to his truck, grabbed his chain saw, and went right back to that house as fast as he could and proceeded to saw that precious pecan wood into rounds and load it into his trailer. Never asked permission or even talked to the homeowners. We noted with a laugh that we had never seen him working so hard.

I observed a lot about fire behavior at 34's, simply because we made so many fires. I have seen fire almost have "arms" or something like that. I really don't know how to describe it, but on several occasions, I would be in a house fire pulling a hose at a doorway or corner and see fire burning on the wall literally "reach out" at my guys as they went by, only to return to the wall after they'd passed. I know; it sounds weird, but I have seen it with my own eyes several times.

In the front yard on RIT (rapid-intervention team) duty at a house fire one night, I saw fire, which was coming out of a ground-story window directly in front of me, go from the usual irregular lapping to a perfect cone shape, almost like a horizontal tornado, about ten feet long. The sideways "fire-nado" was hollow, and you could see perfectly all the way from the outside end to the other end deep inside the house. I guess there was some wind current from crews ventilating the house that caused it, but it was incredible to watch.

I will close my Station 34 chapter with a word or two on my district chief. Without a doubt, one of the best chiefs I had ever worked for in my career. He was the son of a former fire chief of HFD and straight-up old school. He always sat in a chair against the wall in the kitchen and only said about ten words a day. He picked his teeth with a toothpick, listened, and laughed at all of the bull crap being talked around him.

The chief was always called to dinner first, followed by the senior captain, then the captain, and so forth down the line. We rookies were last, and by the time we were called to get our plates, the chief was pretty much done with his meal. So that meant, before you loaded your plate, and sometimes in the middle of the process, the chief would get up to put his plate in the sink, and one of us rookies better meet him there and wash his plate. It was just a respect thing.

As a rookie, if you needed to talk to the chief, you better follow your chain of command and go through the captain. The chief would do the same, and the only times I heard him talk to me or the other rookie was when he called us into his office for some reason or gave us a direct order.

I remember being at Station 32 one time and answering the fire phone. It was my chief, and I answered the proper way—"Station 32, Simmons." He asked to speak to the captain. I transferred the call and, about six seconds later, heard the captain over the loudspeaker say, "Simmons, go back to Station 34." Even though I had answered the phone, the chief was just old school like that and would only relay information to me through the captain. He was not mean or a jerk—far from it. He just "grew up" in a different HFD atmosphere and was a holdover from those days.

I did not resent it at all and actually liked the separation of the cadre from the men. It is how it is supposed to be, in my opinion. Our captains never once went into the dorm room to get someone or for any other reason. They always sent one of the men into the dorm. I asked why one day and was told by my captain that the dorm belonged to the men and that it was the one and only place that was that way. Everything else belonged to the captain. Call me weird, but I appreciate old traditions like that.

I remember holding the watch while my chief caught a fire call to the next district over and returned late into the night. On two separate occasions, he came to the watch office and told me to sweep out the leaves that had blown into the bay when the bay door was open. Both times, it was about 3:00 a.m.—"Yes sir, Chief." I learned this was a common thing as he had awakened others on the watch to do the same thing many times.

I am glad that he was my chief during my rookie year and that I was able to absorb some of the older ways of the fire department. He was always completely fair to everyone, and everyone respected him.

Chapter 3

Station 26

After my probationary year was up at Station 34, I started looking around for a station that was closer to my house. At the time, I lived in Clear Lake, south of Houston, and was traveling all the way to the north side of Houston to go to work. Station 26 was only about fifteen minutes from my house down on the south side of town, and it looked as if I could get the position, even with my lack of seniority.

It was at Station 26 that I worked with my first female who was part of my crew and not just filling in for the day. She had about five to six years' seniority on me and was a pediatric intensive care nurse "on the side." She had a degree from Cornell University and was one of my favorite people to talk to at the station. She has since quit HFD and is doing full-time nursing now.

I had heard all kinds of stories about working with females in the firehouse, ranging from romances to absolute hatred between males and females. And yes, it was strange the first time I was at the urinal and she walked in saying, "Don't turn around," and went straight to a stall and did her business. In fact, it was strange every time she did that, but it was the only bathroom in the station for her to use, and she told me that she did not want to have to hold it every time she needed to go. I understood and never said anything about it again.

Station 26 is off Dixie Drive near Telephone Road, down near Hobby Airport on the south side of town. I am sure, at one time, this area was a solid middle-class part of town, but when I transferred there, it was run-down and not what it used to be. Thousands of apartments surround the airport area. Ask any fireman or cop; cheap apartments usually are 911-call magnets, and 26's was one of the hotter stations I worked. To add to the run total, Station 40 was being remodeled, and 26's had to cover 40's still alarm also. The only time in my career I made three "working" fires—actual fires that require deploying hose lines and "working" to put them out—in one day was at 26's, and there were several days I made two working fires per shift. It was a good place to fight fire.

Old Lady in Bed

People always ask if I have ever saved anyone from a burning building. The vast majority of fires I have been on do not have a victim, and that is a good thing. But the short answer to that question is yes; however, there needs to be some explanation about what happened. One time,

I helped get a downed firefighter, who was out of air, out of a large house fire. Another time, I actually picked up an old lady from her bed as her house was on fire. I have also helped pull out deceased victims from structure fires and have worked victims who were declared later. In addition, I have been at fires in which no one even knew there was a victim until after the fire was out and overhaul had started. My best friend and his crew once stepped over a huge fire's rubble pile for over an hour before a body was discovered under it. It is not pleasant or often, but it happens. Making the "movie star" save by grabbing a victim and walking out onto the front yard with a grateful victim hugging your neck does happen, but it's a once-in-a-career-type save.

The most common occurrence is finding an unconscious victim near a doorway, your crew and you working together to drag out the victim, depending on their size and weight, and handing them over to the paramedic crews who care for them on the front lawn or in the driveway.

Having said all this, I can actually say I picked up an elderly lady from her bed, cradled her in my arms, and handed her through a bedroom window to another firefighter outside. It was quite anticlimactic, and I thought nothing much about it, really, until once again I saw people getting valor awards for doing the exact thing I had done. Is not getting people out of their burning houses part of our job description?

I was on Ladder 26 that day, and we made another house fire. It was a single-story building with the front-right section of the house on fire, heavy smoke visible. Being on the first-in ladder truck, our job was to do the primary search while the pumper crew came in with the hose and made their way to the seat of the fire with intent to extinguish. Smoke was starting to bank down in the house, and the hose crew went to the right towards the kitchen; we went down the hall to the left towards the bedrooms. These were the days before thermal imagers, but visibility was still pretty good.

I opened the door to the last bedroom on the left, and there was a woman who appeared to be sleeping in her bed. At the same time, I noticed someone from Ladder 29 busting out the window in her room from the outside. I yelled at him that I had a victim and was coming out the window with her. He cleaned the glass from the edges of the window with his axe, while I went to her bed and picked her up in my arms as if she were a child. She could not have weighed more than ninety pounds. She woke up at this point, and I remember saying something to try to calm her, but I can only imagine what shock she felt at waking up to being picked up by a fully bunkered-up fireman and carried across her room. I carefully handed her through the window to the guy from 29's and then turned around to rejoin my crew and continue searching the house.

From what I heard later, the other fireman carried her around the house to the front lawn and truly had a "movie" moment. We both had a good laugh at that later on.

We Need a Backboard

Ever since man was created, there has been some form of law enforcement and some form of criminal element, and the two have had violent run-ins; this will never stop as long as the two exist. Being a firefighter, we get the opportunity to uniquely interact in these situations. The most common way is trying to stop the bleeding of whoever has the gunshot holes in them.

I remember one particular run on E26. A thug had fought with a policeman, tried to get the cop's gun, and was shot twice by the police officer, if I remember correctly, in the chest. The call did not come in as a shooting, and we just thought that the police needed us to address wounds on a perp due to a scuffle, as often happens. Engine 26 was called to the scene, and as we arrived, two police officers were still trying to handcuff the guy as all three wrestled on the ground. We helped them hold the guy and secure him while we looked him over for our initial assessment. The perp was still fighting, even while bleeding out due to two holes in his chest. Most of our attention was on the patient as we started to dress his wounds with occlusive dressings to control the bleeding.

HFD protocol at the time was to C-spine immobilize and backboard any gunshot wound. Captain told me to go to the pumper to get the backboard, as the medic unit had not arrived yet, so I stood up and noticed for the first time that a large crowd had gathered and was starting to look and sound agitated. Because, you know, the police just go around shooting anyone and everyone for no good reason, or at least that is what some people think.

This was one time that I remember my senses being on high alert and another time that I believe the prayers of my mother protected me from harm. I had to physically push my way through an angry crowd to get to the back of the pumper, where the backboard was located. As I made it through the main body of people, several very unhappy-looking fellows followed me to the tailboard, watched me climb up into the hose bed and get the backboard, surrounded me, and bumped and pushed me as I carried it back to the scene about twenty-five yards away. I knew they were just waiting for me to say something to set them off; then they would have attacked and fed off each other's rage. Neither my crew nor the cops would have even known until after the damage was done.

I reentered and waded through the main crowd, back to the scene with the backboard. I was very relieved when I reached the patient who was fading fast but still trying to wrestle us as we packaged him for the ride to the hospital. A few minutes later, cops came out of the woodwork, as is usual for a shooting, and secured the scene.

After the medic unit arrived and rushed off to Ben Taub Hospital, I mentioned to my crew what happened, and they told me the crowd had started to get them worried as well. Our backup could not have come fast enough.

I remember making eye contact with one man in particular on the way to the back of the pumper. He had a look of pure hatred in his eyes, and I could tell he saw anyone in uniform as someone he hated, never mind the fact I was trying to help his friend by getting him ready to be rushed to the hospital.

Bag O'Cash

In HFD, because of the type of shift work we do, we have to work an extra day every fifth week; it's called a "debit day." The debit day is universally hated by HFD members for several reasons, but mainly because it falls right in the middle of your days off and for some reason seems to always fall on a day you need off, such as a kid's birthday, a football game, or the like. On your debit day, you are usually an extra man and will be sent out to other stations across the city to wherever manpower is needed. While at Station 26, I did all of my debit days at Station 46 because they were always short on manpower.

One such day, I volunteered to drive M46. This was early in my career when the box did not bother me so much. True to M46's typical days, we were busy the entire twenty-four hours.

We made a call after midnight for an unknown problem about a mile from the station. We arrived to find a Honda Civic still running but standing still in the middle of the road. We were the first on the scene, so we got out to see what was going on and found a young man sitting behind the wheel with his eyes wide open and breathing but completely catatonic, unresponsive to any stimuli. His foot was on the brake, so we put the car in Park and turned it off. While trying to get vital signs on the kid, we noticed a brown paper bag on the passenger seat. A brown paper bag stuffed full of cash. That is when I knew for sure that no one had bothered to help this guy before we stopped because that cash, for sure, would have been taken if they had.

HPD arrived about this time, and as we were loading the stoned patient onto the stretcher, the female officer picked up the bag of cash and complained that now she had to count it and be held accountable for all the cash in the bag, which we guessed was about ten thousand dollars.

I made a joke by saying, "Well, you don't have to count ALL of it," to which I received a serious look in return. My partner and I just laughed it off and proceeded to drive the patient to the hospital.

The Fiery Rat

There was one particular dumpster off Telephone Road that people seemed to enjoy setting on fire, and probably still do. We had to put this dumpster out several times a month and almost always after midnight. We all knew whoever set it on fire was probably watching us put it out from somewhere and enjoying the show.

There are multiple ways to put out a dumpster fire. I have had captains who wanted us to be fully bunked up and pull a hand line, captains who just used the redline, a spooled rubber hose used for small jobs, and a captain who wanted to sit in the truck and use the deck gun on top of the pumper to completely fill the dumpster with water as if it were a big bathtub. Our pumper at 26's did not have a redline, so we used the front "trash line" that sits in a well in the front bumper. The trash line is usually one hundred feet of older hose; much like the redline, it is used on small stuff.

The female on our crew—we will call her Mandy—was on the pumper with me; she was seated behind the driver and riding plugs. I was on first line; it was my job to grab the nozzle and go put the wet stuff on the red stuff.

So we arrive, and, sure enough, the dumpster is full of fire once again. I start pulling the trash line while Mandy is getting a pike pole to move or "stir" the garbage around while we are wetting it. At the dumpster, I knocked down the flames, and as Mandy started to move the trash around, she let out a loud, startled yell and ran back a few feet. I quickly looked over in time to see a moving flame jump up towards her, leap out of the dumpster, and run across the parking lot. A rat in the dumpster probably was covered in cooking oil or grease; it caught fire and decided to jump ship right in front of Mandy. I looked back at the pumper, where the captain and engineer were sitting in the cab, and they had tears in their eyes from laughing so hard.

I can't blame Mandy for jumping back; a rat jumping at you is bad enough, but a rat on fire, not stopping for anyone in its path, is indeed a startling moment. It's funny to me that out of all the things we see in the fire service, I can still recall mindless events like this one.

Find the Hose Line

Just the other day in a training class we were attending, a class to learn how to extricate pilots from downed airplanes, the instructor asked if any of us in the room had ever been lost in a fire and experienced brief moments of panic. I have been asked questions like this by civilians also, and I usually answer with some kind of generic reply because, to the normal person, it really is a difficult question. There is always some small level of fear at any house fire I make. Any fireman who says differently is trying to play macho and is not being honest. It is not the kind of fear that keeps one from doing his job, but rather it is almost as if someone flipped a switch that makes you instantly shift from goofing around to go time. I really am not sure how to explain it any better than that.

I have always told my sons that courage is not the absence of fear, but rather courage is being afraid and doing it anyway. Jesus said, "Fear not, for I am with thee." And I take that literally.

To be honest with myself—and the reader, for that matter—there was one time in a house fire when I had to sit back on my knees and force myself to think. I have made belowground, confined-space rescues, and I have been on rope forty-five stories aboveground. I have had regulators malfunction while I'm inside a fire, and I have been in forest fires when the wind has shifted the wrong way. I have suffered minor burns in several very hot fires in which my face mask started to melt. In all these instances, there was always the small fear I mentioned above. But the time I remember having to actually stop, regroup, and think was at a fire when at 26's, and that call really was not an unusual one.

It started as a large but "normal" house fire in a detached garage. No big deal. We started putting the garage out—that's what we do. We soon discovered that there was a gas line feeding the fire; heat, smoke, and fire were spreading through the crawlspace from the garage to the house itself.

I was reassigned to go with a crew into the house and search for fire in the upstairs bedrooms. I was on the nozzle, and we went in the front door; the stairs were just inside to the right. It was night; there was a lot of smoke banking down as we advanced up the stairs. I got to the top of the stairs with the nozzle, and we found more smoke banking down and a tremendous amount of heat. The kind of heat that makes the skin in the bend of your knees and around your pack straps, where your gear is tight on your skin, begin to sting.

I know what this kind of heat means, so I opened up the nozzle to a fog to cool the room down. Then I kneeled with the nozzle on a fog pattern, pointing up at the ceiling, while the others started pulling Sheetrock. Someone pulled a piece in the ceiling, and it must have admitted oxygen to the stacked-up heat behind the wall; flames lit up the room. I thank the Lord that I was already cooling the room when this happened, or things would have gotten much worse.

I aimed the nozzle at the fire, and the room went black again when a guy from 29's yelled that one of the crew was out of air, overcome by the intense heat, and needed to leave right away; he wanted me to lead them out while they carried / dragged out the overcome fireman.

No problem, I said to myself. *The door is right at the bottom of the stairs.* I led the retreat down the stairs amid thick black smoke and turned to my left to what should have been an open door and a quick exit. But when I got to the bottom of the stairs, with the guys still a few feet behind me, and to where the exit was supposed to be, it was not there. I put the nozzle down and started feeling all over the wall to find the door. I could not find it. I felt around again, saying to myself, *I know it is right here! What is going on?*

I moved a few feet and felt some more. Still nothing. The crew behind me was almost to the bottom of the stairs, and a feeling of panic, if only for a second, hit me because it was up to me to find the exit for my guys. I clearly remember sitting back on my heels, making myself calm down, and telling myself to *THINK!* It was then that my very basic training came back, and I thought, *Find the hose. Of course... find the hose to find your way out to safety.*

Now, writing this, it may seem as if this took several minutes, but in reality, all of this went through my head in a matter of probably five seconds. I reached out in the pitch black and felt along the floor, knowing that the hose line leading out could be no other place than in front of me. I found the hose, turned left, and found that somehow or by someone the front door was closed, and it had jammed on the hose, kinking the door shut. My hands found the inch of gap still left between the door jamb and door, and it felt as if I ripped the door open just as I felt the guys bump up behind me. It was a very beautiful sight to see the lights of the pumper through the smoke and dark of night and to know that we were all good.

We got the crew member to the front lawn and took care of him as the chief pulled a second alarm. The fire, of course, was eventually put out, and everything turned out fine.

We went back the next day on shift to look at the house and discuss things. In the light of day, you could see gloved handprints sliding across the few feet of soot-covered wall and on the back of the door where my hands were trying to find the exit. All I knew was that, somehow, the door shut while we were upstairs, and in the smoke and heat, the simple act of finding our entry point became complicated.

As I said, the entire thing probably took less than a minute from the time we started heading down the stairs to the time I reopened the door, but as so many other people have stated in similar situations, it seemed much longer.

Dead Plug

The best firemen I have known in my career have always been guys who were able to think on their feet and quickly produce an alternative to a situation when the original solution does not solve the problem. Changing tactics on a fire, malfunctioning equipment, changing haul systems on a rescue quickly, and reassigning jobs to people who can do it better during go time are all examples of this.

"You are not paid to think" is what rookie firefighters are told time and time again. "You are paid to stay right beside the captain and do what he tells you to do." Well, that only goes so far, and in particular, when you are the only one in the back of the box with a patient, even the greenest of rookie firefighters has to act with autonomy. When there is no one to suggest alternatives, you have to go with your best-educated guess.

I had just been released from my rookie probation when I transferred to Station 26. I had driven the pumper a few times, but other than small kitchen fires or car fires, I had not "pumped" on real fires that much. Honestly, thinking back, I cannot remember whether or not this next incident was my first "real pumping" on a house fire. I don't think it was, but it was surely close. It was, for sure, the first fire I had to think on my feet and act outside of the normal way of doing things. Our captain must have called in or been on vacation that day.

Mandy did not like to drive the pumper, so I was riding in the E/O's spot for the shift. We caught a house fire on the far side of our territory, across Mykawa Road towards 35's area. Engine 35 arrived just before we did, and they "brought their own water" (stopped, hooked up to a hydrant, and drove to the house laying their own supply hose instead of having the second-in pumper do it). I spotted the pumper about twenty yards ahead of 35's and jumped out to help my guys get the tools they needed to go in and do the primary search. It was then the captain told us to pull a line because the hydrant 35's caught was a "dead plug" (not working), and they were going to have to drag hose another block to catch another plug. The house is blowing and going while all of this is happening.

So we stretched the attack line, and I put the truck into pump gear to get my guys water. Engine 26, the second-in engine, was now the "workhorse" (the engine pumping the water) at the fire. Knowing that our engine only carries

500 gallons of water and that there was not going to be any hydrant hooked up to me for several minutes, I started going over options in my head.

By the time the tank read 50-percent full, I gave a report over the radio and had a plan. I had the third-in engine—and, honestly, I forget which exact engine it was—pull up next to me, put his engine in pump gear, and leave it in idle while I hooked his pump's supply hose to my intake on the captain's side. I opened both valves and did a technique called "nurse-tending" my pumper. In less than a couple of minutes, I had 500 more gallons going into my pumper for my guys inside the house to use.

A couple of minutes later, the new hydrant had been caught, and the supply hose was brought to me. I "stabbed"(inserted) my driver-side intake with the hose carrying the hydrant water. Once this was done, all that I needed to do was listen to the radio and monitor the pump panel.

The fire was put out, and when my solution was observed, several guys and the chief came over and told me, "Good job." In the grand scheme of things, it really was not that complicated a solution or that big a deal to figure out. It was a test of my ability to think quickly and solve a problem; I was simply relieved that I passed and that the Lord helped me act without having to go ask someone what to do.

There was one other thing that I remember about this fire. Once the supply hose was unhooked from 35's pumper—and

I think they were in a reserve (backup) pumper at the time—the firefighter "riding up" (driving) that day did not take it out of pump gear. The tank-to-pump valve was closed, and that means the pump was running the entire time without any water in it, so the pump was getting hotter and hotter. By the time the fire was out and the crews were outside, white smoke was wafting up through the pump panel. The acting E/O ran over there and immediately killed the engine. That was the first and only time I saw smoke coming from an engine's pump.

Idiot Husband

Many times in life, the actions of stupid people don't actually end up causing them harm or discomfort; rather, the people around them pay the price. One such call angered me to the core because of what happened to the moron's wife.

We were called to a house for burns, and we arrived to find a poor lady with first- and second-degree burns to her face, neck, and parts of her scalp where her hair had been burned off. She was obviously in great pain, and with burns on the face, the EMT must be concerned with airway problems in case the victim inhaled fire or intense heat, either of which could damage their airway. I was on the pumper when the medic unit arrived and immediately loaded her and started to administer pain meds.

The police arrived and started to question the husband. This complete idiot was out of lighter fluid and had the bright idea of starting his grill with gasoline. So he lights some paper in the grill and tries to pour a little gas onto the charcoal with a small gas can. Sure enough, the gas lights with a fireball. The spout on the small gas can catches on fire, and this genius decides that the best way to put that out is to sling it to his right, which threw flaming fuel right into the face of his poor wife who was standing there. After hearing his story, there wasn't one of us who did not want to punch this guy right in his stupid head.

Pray Without Ceasing

Growing up the son of a Methodist preacher, I have a pretty good idea about how most church services go. I can count on one hand how many times I missed church as a kid. Heck, we even went to church when on vacations. One Sunday at 26's, we made a check-for-smoke call to a church, during the middle of their service, and they weren't going to let a little smoke stop their singing.

We arrived and heard the praise music before we even walked into the building. The scene was a very typical setting for praise and worship in the majority of Black churches across America—very lively, very loud, and very joyful.

The preacher came down from the stage and met us halfway down the aisle while the singing and band kept on. There was light smoke coming out of one of the vents in the ceiling, which was a raised ceiling about twenty feet high. While the captain started scanning with the thermal imager, the custodian of the church offered us the ladder he used to change bulbs.

So we set it up, right in the middle of the church, with praise and worship not skipping a beat, and lifted ceiling tiles to look for more smoke and/or fire. The preacher went back up to the stage and carried on with the service. While we were looking and checking, he danced down every few minutes to ask for an update.

After about fifteen minutes, we finally determined that one of the air blowers had a burned-out motor; we shut off the power to that fan and explained it to the custodian and preacher. Praise and worship had been going on the entire time. We put the ladder back outside the sanctuary, grabbed our gear, and walked down the aisle to the exit to the drumbeat and clapping of the praise and worship that never ceased the entire fire call.

Flipping Out

I was riding first line on Engine 26 one shift when we received a fire call to a gas explosion in a residence. We were the second-in engine company, so our job was to catch the plug. Our driver stopped near a hydrant down the block from the address of the fire, and the firefighter riding plugs got off the pumper to hook up to the hydrant.

The process of catching the plug is not complicated, as it is a basic skill that everyone masters before leaving the academy. Already with your fire gear on, you step off the truck, walk to the tailboard of the pumper, and grab the female coupling end of the supply hose from the hose bed. You next pull enough supply hose off the truck to reach the hydrant and wrap a few feet around the hydrant, your foot holding the hose in place. You then signal the driver to go. The truck will pull up to the first-in truck, and the supply line you just laid is attached to the first-in engine's pump. While this is happening, the "plug man" removes the hydrant cap on the front of the hydrant, attaches the hose to it, and waits for the signal to turn the water on.

As stated before, the usual way to anchor the hose to the hydrant as the pumper drives away is to wrap it around the hydrant and hold it down with your foot. After the driver saw Mandy's signal to go, he hit the gas and a few seconds later started yelling and laughing very loudly. He yelled, "She flipped," but I was too busy putting my gear on to pay much attention at the time.

I later found out why he was laughing so hard. Instead of wrapping the hose around the hydrant, for some reason, Mandy must have just stood with two feet on the hose and given the signal to go. The truck took off, and a coupling from the hose bed caught coming off the bed. It completely pulled the carpet out from under her feet. I was told she did a complete flip right in front of Ladder 29's crew, who were pointing and almost falling down, laughing...all while a house fire was raging on.

As for the gas explosion, it caused complete and total devastation. The call came in, in the middle of the afternoon, so the residents were thankfully at work, but they returned to a house that was simply gone and replaced by a burning pile of rubble. Sheets of plywood were twenty feet up in the large oak trees, and not a single wall was left standing. It was one of the easier house fires I made because it simply was a burning pile of wood and debris.

"Is This Guy Serious?"

One Sunday morning, we made a syncope (fainting) call to a church with a congregation that was mainly, or all, Black folks. We arrived to find an elderly man lying on the floor of the church. Upon initial exam, he presented with no pulse. We had the jump bag and oxygen with us, and I immediately went out to the truck to get the AED while CPR was started on the man.

I grabbed the AED and started back to the door of the church at a very fast pace. As I passed a few people, one man shouted at me, "I bet if you were in Bellaire"—an upper-class White neighborhood of Houston—"you would be running." He was implying that since I was White and the patient was Black, somehow that made a difference to me, so I was just taking my time.

My first reaction was to look at him while I passed by and to think to myself, *Is this guy serious?* There was no time to even address the guy, as we had a cardiac arrest on the floor.

We placed the pads on the patient and hit Analyze to see if he was in a shockable rhythm. He was, and on the second set of shocks, we got pulses back. The medic unit showed up, loaded him, and transported him to the hospital, where we learned later that he was in serious-but-stable condition.

After we were done with all of the patient care on the scene, I looked around to see if the man who had spoken to me was still around, as I was going to confront him. I at least wanted to let him know that we do not treat anyone any differently, no matter what neighborhood they come from. I, and every fireman with whom I have ever worked, have proven this many times throughout the years. I also wanted to let him know that this fireman he thought was so racist just saved his friend's life. But, alas, he was gone, and it was probably for the best.

I am a professional. So are my coworkers. That is all I really need to say.

Chapter 4

Leaving HFD

After three years in HFD, I started to wonder if there was another career out there that I could try, one in which I could use my degree and not deal with people who dialed 911 for every issue in their lives. Yes, the EMS system bothered me that much. I could not get over why people did not take care of themselves, instead of wanting someone else to come in and do it for them.

Here I was, still living in Houston—which I hated—with a forestry-related degree, so I started looking around at those types of jobs. I came across the Texas Forest Service website and sent a few emails just to see what was out there. I was eventually put in contact with the Wildland Firefighting division of the service and was invited up to Granbury, Texas, to meet with them and check it out.

I arrived and met several fine folks who proceeded to conduct an interview session right then and there. I guess I passed because, that day, they offered me a position as a regional fire coordinator based in San Antonio. It sounded like a dream job. I would cover what was then the DPS

Region 3, which consisted of fifteen counties from Comal County down to the border. This offered me a chance to move to the Hill Country and raise my kids there. So I decided to leave HFD and pursue a career in forestry firefighting.

One thing I did not know about the Texas Forest Service is that it is part of the state's incident-command team on all large-scale state responses. During the interview, I was told to expect "some" travel. What should have been said is to expect *to be home* "some" of the time, and being on the incident-command team had much to do with that.

It was not long before I realized I had made a mistake in joining the forest service. Matter of fact, it was probably the first week, when I met the fire coordinator who was going to be doing my training. When I took the job, I was under the impression that I would be traveling around my fifteen counties, checking on their needs, and also coordinating state resources and local assets during an emergency within my territory. I would be away from home for training, conferences, or emergencies that occurred only every once and a while—"some" travel. Sounded great to me, but when I was meeting with the member who was to oversee me, I learned that "some" travel was not the case; he was almost never home and seemed to like it that way. His dedication to his job was irrefutable, but his dedication to his family was in dire need of help, in my opinion. I asked him if being away from home three weeks every month caused problems with his family. He responded that his kids got to see him "when they could."

I had a wife I loved and two little boys who were my main focus in life. Boys need Dad to be home and to be a father, and any man who chooses a career over raising his sons is no one I will take any advice from on any subject. It was made plain to me that this type of travel would be expected of me also. It was this conversation, along with being in a hotel room so many nights that it went way beyond "some," that started me on my journey to New Braunfels Fire Department.

The is not to say that there were no good or even great people in the Texas Forest Service. The actual job of meeting people and doing fire work was great. I have said many times that the fire-coordinator job I had would have been perfect for a single guy with no kids…perfect, just not for me.

Teach?

I have always had a problem with the fire service and any other organization that puts people through a class and then sends them out to teach the class. No real-world experience in the field and you want them to teach others?

Well, this happened to me. I went through the basic Wildland Firefighter class, S130/190 training, did my "pack test" (timed test with a loaded backpack), and earned my red card (Wildland Firefighter certification). As a sidenote, I found it humorous that the "dedicated" guy in charge of me could not pass the pack test and therefore held no red card. It is always the loudest barkers, isn't it?

So now that I had my "quals," the service sent me to teach the class to departments in my area. *Teach? I just passed it last week, have no field experience in fighting wildland fires, and you want me to go teach?* I brought this up to one of my bosses, and he said he understood my concern, but the answer was yes.

I HAVE NEVER AGREED WITH THIS. At a fire department for which I worked part-time, there were two brand-new rookies who just graduated from their fire academy not even two months earlier and had ZERO house fires under their belts, but they went back to help teach at the academy from which they just graduated. What are they going to teach? Are they going to draw from their vast years of experience fighting fires? Of course not. They did as I did when I was forced to teach—although they volunteered —and they taught the book just as they had learned a few weeks earlier. Makes zero sense to me.

Because of my concerns, I was able to join the guys in Bastrop doing several hundred acres of prescribed burns out at Camp Swift, and I was grateful. I was able to observe how forest fires behave, how wind affects fires, how humidity affects fires, and how a fire line and backing fires work. It was great and one of the months that I truly loved. Just being out in the woods is great…and then you get to burn stuff? Awesome.

Pine Mountain

While in the Texas Forest Service, the biggest fire I was assigned to was outside of Fort Davis on Pine Mountain, near the observatory. This was both a miserable experience and a good one in which I got to observe and be part of a large event for which hotshot crews from around the nation were called in to help. I believe it was also the first fire in Texas in which crews heli-rappelled into the areas.

I had just bought some new White's wildland boots. Some of the best that you can buy and will last a long time, but take some miles to break in. No problem, as I had a way to wear the stiffest of boots without a problem; I had perfected the technique back in basic training. I was one of the few who never developed a single blister in sixteen weeks of basic due to the fact I wore polypropylene liners under the wool socks we were issued. This lets the boots slip on the polypro socks and not your skin, therefore preventing blisters. Near the end of basic, my secret was out, and there was a lot of bargaining by guys for me to lend them extra pairs of my polypro liners.

So there should have been no problem going to this fire with new boots, as I had done this before. The problem was, when I got there, I discovered that I had forgotten my polypro socks, and we were up in the mountains, away from any town that would sell such things. Not much choice but to wear the new boots and hope for the best.

Well, the best did not happen—in fact, the worst did. We were assigned about a six-mile hike up a canyon to light a backfire, and we were to keep dripping fire on the fire line all the way back down. About twelve miles over rough terrain. Usually, this is the kind of thing I drool over. It was a beautiful canyon and nice weather. But about thirty minutes in, on my heels, I started to feel the hot spots warning me of what was coming. So I slowed it down a little, which put me behind the guys slightly. Thirty minutes later, I had straight-up blisters on my heels, and walking hurt with every step. I stopped to try to doctor my feet some, and that put the guys way ahead of me. I heard one guy say to the chief later that he turned around, but I wasn't there. Made me wonder if he even wondered or cared what happened to me.

I took off my socks to try to put some Band-Aids on my heels, but the damage was done. I had deep, bleeding blisters about the size of a quarter on each heel, and when the air hit the raw skin, it felt as if my heels were on fire. I patched them up the best I could and continued slowly, knowing that I would, at the very least, catch the rest of the guys on the way back.

It was about four more hours of painful walking before I finally met them coming back down. I did my best to ignore the pain, grabbed a drip torch, and started dropping fire where we needed it. It was about three more hours of walking back at a pace much faster than I should have walked and with intense pain every single step.

Blisters are one of those little things that will absolutely ruin your day if you let them manifest themselves. When you suck it up and drive on, you make them worse. But you have a job to do, so you just have to "Charlie Mike" (continue the mission).

Late that night, when we finally got to the command post, I very tenderly removed my boots and bloody socks. I had the two deepest, most painful blisters that I had ever had in my entire life, about the size of a quarter on each heel. I was amazed at how painful they were. All because I did not take care of my business and pack the right gear —no one to blame but me. Quite a first day.

I doctored the blisters the best I could and tried to get a few hours of sleep. When I woke up, as blisters usually do, they hurt even worse on the second day. To make matters worse, a runny nose I had been fighting for a few days had become a full-blown sinus problem. My nose was stopped up, my ears were too, and I had a major headache to boot. So there I was...completely miserable...each step a new adventure in pain...blowing out green and yellow stuff from my nose...with a pounding head. To put it simply, I was hurting and pretty sure I had a fever.

That day, I was assigned to the "track engine" (an old Army M113 armored transport that had been converted into a brush truck) with a guy who was a twenty-plus-year veteran in the forest service. An M113 is a very loud, bumpy vehicle, and it simply made my head hurt worse. I'm sure

I let a complaint about something slip out, and the guy heard it. He let me know that he was not the one giving the orders, and it was our job just to do it. It was exactly what I needed to hear to snap me out of my current state. I immediately apologized, told him I was sick, said he was right, and once again said I was sorry for the comment. I was miserable, but that was no excuse for complaining.

This was and still is a chapter in my life that I regret. I allowed my personal circumstances in life to interfere with completing the mission and getting the job done. I am ashamed of that to this day.

Later that day, I found a local townsperson and asked for two pairs of the thinnest dress socks she could find in town and some sinus medication. The next day, I was taken off the track engine, either as a blessing from the Lord, or the older guy went to the boss and said, "Take this guy off my engine." It was probably both. I had some cold medicine in me and bandaged heels covered by dress socks under my regular socks. This was not quite polypro, but it was better than nothing. So I was slightly better by the third day.

My assignment for the next week was to transport a hot-shot team from Mexico named *Los Diablos* from the bottom of the mountain up to the fire on the mountain. This simply meant loading their gear and a few guys in my truck, putting it in four-wheel drive, and off-roading up a jeep trail each day. This really was the Lord looking out for me and an assignment I enjoyed doing even while sick. I was able to practice my Spanish, and several of the guys had interesting stories. Having this team on the fire was not without controversy though. Most Indian reservations in the Rocky Mountain states have fire crews and are very good firefighters. I had one Apache hotshot tell me that they had a sister crew sitting at the reservation, waiting on an assignment, and his crew did not like Los Diablos being used when Americans could be there instead. He had a point, in my opinion.

Controversy aside, Los Diablos were hard workers and cheerful most of the time. Their foreman was a ranger from Big Bend National Park; he parked his truck on a bluff over the Rio Grande, honked his horn, and flashed his lights to spread the word around the villages on the other side that Los Diablos were needed.

After eight days on this fire, my heels were almost back to normal, but the sinus infection was still going strong. The cold meds helped with the headaches, but not much with the stuffed-up sinuses. One guy from Bastrop needed to get home, and I volunteered to take him so I could get to the doctor to get some antibiotics and then return. So we drove to Bastrop, and I returned to New Braunfels. I was gone a week before the fire, home for three days, and then gone again for eight days, but as I was learning, this was typical for the job.

I went to the doctor the next day and received a call later that the fire was under control and being demobilized. There was no need to drive all the way back out to Fort Davis. I was fine with that.

So that was my experience on the Pine Mountain fire. Eight days of not much fun when it should have been a good, solid experience. I did enjoy meeting new people and seeing new country, but not as much as I could have or should have. While there, I tried not to let many people know that I was sick and had bad blisters because that sounds like an excuse; it makes you seem weak. It all started with my lack of properly planning my gear, but I look back on this episode and use it as a stepping stone and lesson on the road to being a better person and doing a better job.

Ice Storm and the Beginning of the End

The call that really made me start pursuing a return to structural firefighting was during the ice storm that hit East Texas in 2001. Once again, being part of the state's emergency-management team, the forest service fire coordinators were called to Tyler to manage the response effort and cleanup after almost two weeks of no power, which was caused by the winter storm.

Laura, my wife, was sick with a fever, my five-year-old had a fever, and his one-year-old little brother needed to be taken care of. I got the call about 10:00 p.m. I needed to get on the road to Tyler ASAP and be there by morning.

Well, I told my supervisor that I was not leaving; I would leave in the morning so that my wife could rest in bed that night while I took care of the boys. This did not sit well with my supervisor, but I did not care in the least. I left the next morning with Laura still running a fever and two boys to care for, and I did not come home until nine days later.

Once there, I was again unit resource leader, and to anyone who is not familiar with the incident-command system, what that means is you sit on your ass in the command post and keep track of where units or resources are and what they are doing. Not my cup of tea—I would rather have been out there slinging a chain saw and clearing roads than stuck in the command post for eight days as reports came in about people stealing railroad generators, taking an axe to the electric company's trucks in retaliation for not restoring power, and price gouging normal goods. When things settled back down, we were released to go home.

Once home, my wife and I talked about applying to the New Braunfels Fire Department as I had become good friends with a member named Darren, who wanted me to apply. Darren and I had earned our red cards together.

A few days after I got home, I received word from the forest service that, the next week, I was going to Florida for twenty-one days. I was done—I told my boss that I would be leaving the forest service and going back to structural firefighting. He said that he kind of had the feeling I was not happy, and it was not a surprise to him. To this day, I hold him in the highest regard. David Abernathy was a good man, and he was also one of the most intelligent men with whom I have ever worked.

I have to admit that it has taken me several days to write this short section on working in the Texas Forest Service. It is a chapter of my life that was bittersweet. I met many fine folks who care about their job and want to help people. I feel as if, when I first applied for the job, I was misled about how much travel and away-from-home time the job actually required, but on the other hand, I look back and know that I could have adjusted my attitude and made it better for myself. There was a time in my life when all that travel would have fit me just fine. But at that season in my life, that was not what I was looking for, and life is way too short to stay for too long in a position that does not suit your current situation. If things aren't right, change those things...and I did.

Chapter 5

New Braunfels Fire Department

Taking the advice of my friend Darren, I applied to New Braunfels Fire Department and eventually was hired. Up to that point, my only experience in the fire-department world was with the huge Houston Fire Department and teaching wildland classes at small departments here and there. This was my first time being a member of a small department—eighty-six members at the time—and I really never thought there would be any difference. I was wrong, very wrong.

The call volume, or lack thereof, was the first difference. Being used to ten to fifteen calls a day, EVERY DAY, I was taken aback at how much time we had around the station. In HFD, if you talked a big game, you better be able to back it up because "The Truth" was coming, and he had your name on his list. You can only brag so long about how good you are because a fire is always just a few hours or short days away, and everyone will soon see if you have the right stuff or not.

Because New Braunfels was known as "No Burnfels" at the time, many of the members poured themselves into being "super medics" because there were always plenty of chances to perform EMS. They were very good at their jobs, and still are today.

Let me say this—God bless guys who just love EMS. I don't. I started out in the fire service actually wanting to be a paramedic, and, the first two years or so on the box, I had a lot of fun. But I eventually got to the point, like most big-city EMTs, that I dreaded taking care of people who should be taking care of themselves. Honestly, the current system just beats you down to your knees. To this day, I believe that fire, EMS, and police should be three separate city divisions. EMS has absolutely nothing to do with fighting fire and vice versa. But, alas, it is part of the job, and everyone has to do their time on the box.

Not so much anymore, but when I joined NBFD, there were still a lot of the local German old guard in the department. It was made known to me very early that I was an auslander, or outsider, since I was not a descendant of the original Germans who founded the town, nor was I born there. I also caught flak from some of the old guard for being from Houston. Most of the guys absolutely hated people from Houston. Not HFD, but people who live in the city of Houston. It was not until my first summer working there that I understood why. It seemed as if every drunk tourist who caused us so much trouble on the river had an address in Houston, Conroe, Katy, etc.

One small example I can remember about the difference between HFD and NBFD happened during training. I caught the plug, and after turning the hydrant on, I walked back to the scene with the hydrant wrench and put it back in its place on the pumper. In Houston, you NEVER leave the wrench on the plug because the citizens would either steal it, turn off your water with it, or both. When the training was finished, one guy walked down to the hydrant and started yelling about the wrench not being there. I explained my reasoning for what I did and was told very bluntly that New Braunfels was not Houston. In this, we agreed.

Raging River on Geronimo Creek

At the time, NBFD was not large enough to have a dedicated "heavy" rescue team on duty each shift. The rescue truck was a truck with a dog-catcher's bed (large compartments with doors, similar to what animal control uses) that held extrication tools like the Jaws of Life, ropes, swift-water gear for water rescues, and a few other specialty tools. The truck was manned each shift by two people of the battalion captain's choosing, usually on a rotating basis. These two would leave their current truck assignment, jump on the rescue truck, and make the call.

I was assigned with an NBFD veteran to the rescue truck one shift, and late that night, during heavy rain, we were sent to a truck stalled in high water. We arrived at Alligator Creek and Freiheit Road to find a man sitting in his Toyota truck in much less than a foot of water. My partner and I looked at each other, grabbed the flashlights, and walked out to meet him.

When we opened the door of the truck, the man inside said his truck stalled when he hit the water over the road, so he dialed 911 for help. Meaning, he did not take a moment to assess his situation and determine his next step. My partner asked the man if he was ready to go, but the man had a confused look on his face. So then my partner asked him to step out into the ankle-deep water, which he did. We then proceeded to walk twenty yards back to the rescue truck. We called a wrecker, got the man taken care of, and went back to the station, all the while wondering how some people get through this life without bumping their heads on every single low branch out there.

Later that night, well after midnight, we got another call for a swift-water rescue on a normally calm, small creek towards Seguin named Geronimo Creek. This call was at a low-water crossing out in the county, and we were called to help volunteer units already on scene. Seguin FD boats were already out on calls in the city, so in accordance with mutual-aid agreements, NBFD was sent to assist.

When we arrived on the scene, pulling our rubber rescue boat, there was still a gentle rain falling, and all of the blue and red lights from a dozen fire trucks reflected their colors in the nighttime raindrops at flashing intervals. The normally dry concrete water crossing was an absolute horrendous raging torrent of brown floodwater and debris probably a good four feet above the concrete.

I looked in disbelief as we were given the update that a car tried driving through that raging, angry creek and got swept downstream. Why would anyone try to drive through that? Throughout my career in the fire department, I have always had trouble believing how stupid people can be. Sure, I make mistakes, but for the most part, my friends and I don't make bad, life-changing, or life-ending decisions on a daily basis. Isn't everyone else like that too? The answer is a big, resounding NO. We learned later that one of the victims was found washed down the creek and dead.

Now there are two ways to look at this. One is that these people made a stupid decision to cross a raging torrent of a river, at night, during a flood-storm weather event, and now we have to venture into this extremely dangerous situation and put our lives on the line—and literally a safety line—to save the victims. And there is part of me that agrees with that.

The other way—and MY way of looking at it—is that people are stupid, but now it's go time…and I get to do what I am trained to do. I get to see if I have what it takes to complete the mission, the skill set to do it correctly, the courage to beat down fear and doubt, and Charlie Mike. It is an opportunity to prove your worth, and what more can a man ask for? I get to go out, save a young woman who is up in an oak tree, surrounded by floodwaters, bring her down, and in my boat take her to safety on the shore. The very definition of manhood.

The floodwaters were about sixty yards wide with a group of live oaks in the middle. I am sure that normally the oaks lined the banks of the creek, but now the banks were simply where the water decided they should be. By using spotlights, we could see the woman about ten feet up in the tree and hanging on for dear life. In floods, it is not only the current that is life-threatening, but also the hidden trees, debris, fence lines, etc. that catch people and hold them under. In the rescue world, these obstacles are called strainers, and they work on people exactly as a strainer works on pasta—the water goes through, but the pasta (person) stops.

So this was indeed a life-or-death call and needed to be dealt with right away. We quickly donned our vests and wet suits while others backed the boat up to the water's edge and got it ready to go. The usual procedure for rescuing someone from floodwaters is to go with the current, float past the victim in the tree or whatever, then make a sudden J-turn, and approach from downstream, coming up into the eddy current, a small patch of semi-calm water directly behind the object. Once at the tree, car, or other object they are trapped on, you put the nose of the boat directly onto the object, bow facing upstream, and give the motor gas to keep it straight and in contact with the object. This docking maneuver is called "pressurizing," and it is a coordinated effort between the crew member on the tiller and the rescue man. The rescuer then makes the victim put on a life vest BEFORE coming across the gap to the boat, just in case they fall into the water.

Before we set out, a decision was made to tether the nose of the boat with a rope in case the motor died and we were at the mercy of the water. A boat needs power to steer, and we thought that since this was the Texas Hill Country, there could be thousands of hidden large rocks; the prop could hit one at any time. A leash on the boat would allow men on the shore to pendulum swing the boat back to the bank if we lost power.

The problem with this is it takes constant vigilance by the men on the shore so that they only let out enough slack or take it up quickly, as needed. Very similar to belaying for a rock climber. As in all rescues, the situation will dictate what technique is to be used, and anyone who wants to stand by what the book says every time has never made an actual rescue. Normally, I would not vote for a tether on the boat because, as I stated before, it takes great coordination between shore parties and those in the boat.

The decision was then made to not risk the J-turn for fear of rocks. We would let the boat drift, with the motor in Neutral, to below the tree, and then my partner would put it in gear quickly and power up to the tree to dock it. As I said, the situation dictates.

We were pushed off the bank about fifty yards above the tree, from what is called the river's right bank, as determined by facing downstream. Without much trouble, the guys on the shore slowly lowered us down through the floodwaters until we were about twenty yards below the tree and at about its eight-o'clock position.

I was pumped up from the excitement of it all, but, looking back, this was a very dangerous job. It was the middle of the night, with floodwaters splashing into the boat, in the middle of what were easily class-4 or class-5 rapids of brown, debris-laden muck.

My partner then hit the gas, and we went up below the tree as planned. I was trying to yell instructions to the woman, but she was so scared she climbed down and was almost in the boat before we docked at the tree. I immediately started getting a life jacket on her even though she wasn't listening to me as she scrambled into the boat. My partner was doing a good job of keeping the boat in the tree's eddy current and as stable as could be expected. The actual getting her out of the tree and into the boat probably took only about twenty seconds.

The return trip is where things went a little wrong. Either through lack of planning, lack of situational awareness, or just plain old-fashion lack of communication, as my partner hit full throttle to get us to shore, going at about a 45-degree upstream angle to the bank, the slack in the rope was not taken up fast enough, and the boat went over the rope, and it was sucked into the prop and cut. Of course, the tangle stopped the prop. We were in the worst-case scenario—no motor and no tether to the shore.

By the grace of God, the momentum from the full throttle and the timing of the rope tangle pushed us just past the eddy line into the less severe laminar flow of the bank. Two men were running out to grab the boat, and I could see the water was below knee level, but the current was still swift. I grabbed the girl by the arm and took her out of the boat with me, handed her off to one of the guys, and grabbed the boat handles with the other guy holding on for dear life for my partner. He got out and helped us drag the boat far enough up on the shore, where help was, and we sat down to catch our breath.

If that rope had caught the prop just ten feet earlier, a bad situation would have become much, much worse. As it happened, the prop stopped, but the boat had just enough momentum going to push through the eddy wall to slightly safer water.

While getting out of the wet suits, we received confirmation that another victim was found a few hundred yards downstream. Three victims went in, and only two came out alive.

We loaded up and made it back to the station at about 4:00 a.m. Needless to say, we were both beat at the 7:00 a.m. shift change.

2002 Flood

There are several things I remember most about the 2002 flood—it was the second 100-year flood in four years, I watched an entire home float across the Common Street bridge over the Guadelupe River, and I saw the Canyon Gorge at the lake get created in less than a day. But, you know, it takes millions of years to carve a canyon 150 feet deep. Yeah, right.

One particular task hit me pretty hard. We had to go out to the area around Dry Comal Creek and advise residents to evacuate because of rising floodwaters. There are several homes scattered around, and we needed to talk to as many as we could as fast as we could.

My partner that day and I pulled into a trailer park along the creek and started knocking on doors. I knocked on one door, and a little boy about eight years old answered. I asked for his mother, and she came to the door, wondering why a fireman was at her home. I explained that we were suggesting she evacuate, to grab what she could and move to higher ground. A look of despair mixed with worry appeared on her face. I asked if she had anywhere to go or family to go to, and she said no. It was just she and her son. I informed her that the Red Cross would soon be setting up a shelter and that I had several other homes I needed to inform as quickly as possible, so I had to go.

She looked at me with a face that said, "Please don't leave," and tears started to well up in her eyes. Was she going to lose to a flood the only place she and her boy had? I have to admit, it hit me hard, and I felt a deep sympathy for this mother and son. I stepped back up to the door and simply repeated that she should grab what she could, get to higher ground, and play it safe. I told her that the water may not even reach her home, that this was just a precaution. I looked her in the eye and told her that she needed to do what must be done to keep her boy safe and that it would be all right.

I had several other families to warn and had to leave. I'm not sure why this instance sticks out in my memory. I have seen pain, shock, fear, and sadness, all beyond normal levels, on the faces of hundreds of people over the years. Maybe it was because she was a single mom with a boy and no support to speak of. I hope someday that at least she knows I cared about her and her son's well-being that day.

I am happy to report that I checked on that mobile home park several times during the flood, and the water never came up high enough to flood the homes.

Tailgate Trauma

When I watch shows like *Jackass* and see all of the stunts and crazy things they put their bodies through, I am amazed that more serious injuries don't happen. It almost makes me think that minor accidents are more dangerous than major risky stunts. I have seen people die from small falls and mishaps. But I have also watched the *Jackass* crew do things that look like as if they were trying to kill themselves, and they come out unhurt. I will give one sad example.

While working at Station 2 in NBFD, we were called for a fall on a street only about two blocks from the station. We arrived to find an unconscious teenage girl on the ground, surrounded by a few friends behind a pickup truck. First impression —maybe she is drunk and fell, or something like that.

We got to the patient and asked bystanders what happened. We were told they were goofing around in the truck, and she was standing on the rear bumper when the driver touched the gas, and the truck moved forward suddenly, causing her to fall backward to the street. She slammed her head on the concrete and hadn't moved since. Just like that, our situation got upgraded to critical.

Upon examination, we saw a large hematoma on the back of her head and noticed slurred speech when responding to questions. She was still semiconscious and trying to talk, but not making much sense. The engine crew arrived, and we quickly immobilized her C-spine, while assisting her breathing with the BVM, and loaded her into the box. Air Life was called, and my paramedic partner made the determination to perform RSI (rapid-sequence intubation) while waiting for the chopper to land, as her respirations were going downhill fast.

RSI is a very advanced field procedure, and it requires a crew to be on their A game, for sure. Because of the human gag reflex, a patient who is intubated usually needs to be unconscious to avoid rejection of the tube as it is being shoved down their throat and into their airway. In the RSI process, a paralytic drug is administered that stops the patient from breathing. This allows the tube to be placed while the patient is still conscious. During this process, the patient must be "bagged" (ventilated with the bag-valve mask) with a high flow of oxygen, or the patient will die. The RSI procedure is not routinely done; it is a last-resort tool in the toolbox and only pulled out when needed. NBFD is to be commended for having the foresight and ability to use this in the field.

My partner administered the paralytic, and I bagged the patient—in effect, breathed for her. Even though she was only about halfway up the Glasgow scale, I could see she noticed she couldn't breathe on her own, and it, understandably, bothered her. I made a mental note to concentrate on the bag and tune out everything else going on.

The chopper landed, and we quickly transferred the patient to the air ambulance and informed the crew of the situation.

When my partner first said we were going to RSI the girl, I knew he felt something about the situation, so I needed to go with his decision. It was absolutely the right call, and the simple fall from the tailgate ended up, sadly, killing the girl. The fall resulted in a bleed in the brain that put her in a coma and eventually took her life.

This is why I said what I did about the *Jackass* crew above—they do stunts many times more risky, several times a show, and get a few bruises and maybe a sprained ankle. My heart goes out to the family of this girl, especially the driver whose foot hit the gas and caused the truck to lurch forward. Just a stupid accident.

Man vs. Train: Part Two

Station 2 in New Braunfels has railroad tracks about a quarter mile or so behind the station. The next road down from the station crosses the tracks not too far from where the girl on the truck fell.

Very early one morning, about an hour before shift change, we were hit with a call for a possible train casualty near the crossing. The engineers had called 911 after seeing a man near the tracks in the early morning light. They blew the horn several times and passed close to him, but they did not know whether or not the train hit the man. Needless to say, the impact of a 150-pound man will not be felt up in the wheelhouse of a train if a collision occurs.

I was on the box that day, and we arrived before the engine and started looking for the man. After about ten minutes of looking in the predawn light, we finally found him about 150 yards down from the crossing. There was no blood and gore, as I was expecting and had seen in the past with train incidents, but he definitely did not look right. He was lying on his back about two feet from the tracks.

By this time, the engine was with us too, and we immediately started checking for vital signs. My partner hooked up the EKG while I held the man's C-spine, and that's when I noticed that his head felt as if I were holding a bag of marbles or something like that. There was no bone structure to speak of, and his spine was snapped. Upon further exam, we found the blood in his hair, and with more daylight coming, we could make out bruising and battering marks on the side of his entire head.

The EKG showed a flat-line cardiac rhythm, but his body was still warm, and my partner thought that maybe we should work him. But with a deformed, crushed head, broken neck, and downtime of 20-plus minutes, this was a DOA. I don't blame him for wanting to work the guy because it is in your nature, hopefully, to give everyone a chance, but sometimes reality is just that—reality. It is a difficult part of the job, but as I just said, it IS part of the job.

Waiting for the police to arrive, we put together what might have happened. The train engineer told dispatch that he was standing too close to the tracks and never moved, even after the horn. So we think he was leaning over just enough for the engine to bust his head, but not enough to hit his body. Was it a suicide or an alcohol- or drug-induced stupor? I never heard.

Merry Christmas

Working on Christmas and Christmas Eve now and then is just part of being a firefighter, and call volume does not really go down, as one would hope. One particular call on Christmas Eve at Station 2 is one I will never forget.

I was on the box, and we got a call to do a welfare check on a man who called his ex-girlfriend at an office Christmas gathering and said something to the effect that she was not going to have to worry about him anymore. She dialed 911 fearing the worst, and we got the call.

We arrived at a home to see the lights on, but no one answered the door. We knocked some more while identifying ourselves loudly. After a few more seconds to hear a response, we opened the door ourselves, thinking that perhaps he had taken an overdose and was unconscious on the floor, or something like that. We opened the door slowly, announcing ourselves and staying aware of the situation.

My partner was a police officer as well, and I picked up many a tip from him on situations like this. The first thing we saw was the attic ladder down and a pair of legs, from the knee down, hanging from the attic hole. Pretty obvious he was hanging from the rafters and wanted his ex to find him right when she walked in the door, just as we did.

Dodging the body, we climbed up the steps to examine the patient, and it was apparent he was DOA, even without checking for vital signs. His neck was elongated; his eyes were open, swollen, and bulging; and no blood had been above his neck in a while. Honestly, it was gross and somewhat terrifying to look at, as it looked like a painful death. We cut him down with my knife and hooked up the EKG. A flat line, cold body, and obvious C-spine deformity—DOA.

PD had arrived by then and started looking around the house; they found a suicide note. The note was written to the ex and said that he hoped her love for him would "burn in hell with him." I just stood there for a few seconds after I heard that and thought how cruel that was of him to have her remember this every Christmas. But I guess that was the point.

Double Tap

Another suicide that stands out from the others I made was a call at my other fire job at Bracken Fire Department. The call came in as a gunshot wound, and the details stated the victim was in a vehicle in the driveway of a place of business along the highway.

We arrived to find, sitting in the driver's seat, a young man with two obvious holes in his chest and a handgun down near his hand. Dramatic music, maybe from some movie soundtrack, was playing through the car stereo very loudly, and he was parked where the owners of the place of business would not miss him. The thing that stood out about this suicide was the two shots to his chest.

My first thought was that this was a murder scene, because it is very uncommon for someone to shoot themself in the chest a second time if the first shot did not do the job. One would think the amount of pain and shock from the trauma of a large-caliber round to the sternum would not allow the thought process it takes to put another round in your chest. The most probable thing was that the shock and pain caused a reflex reaction that pulled the trigger again before the gun fell away. Either way, not a peaceful way to go out.

The entire thing surrounding suicide has been, and continues to be, a mystery to me. I can take you to MD Anderson Cancer Center and show you people who are praying for one more day with their families, but here you have someone just throwing away the precious life that God has given them.

HFD Comes Calling

There were, and are, many quality people in the New Braunfels Fire Department. Good guys whom I will see every now and again and have a few laughs with.

It was a combination of things that started me back on a path to HFD. NBFD was not a Civil Service employer at the time, and you worked at the pleasure of the chief. I saw a firefighter of several years get fired for being overweight, and at the same time, the training captain was just as overweight or bigger, but he kept his cushy job. Anyone could be fired for any reason the chief thought of, and there was no recourse for the employee.

NBFD's retirement was through TMRS (Texas Municipal Retirement System) at that time and, quite simply, not even in the same conversation as HFD's retirement package. Also, the road for promotion in the small department was very limited, as compared to a large department. NBFD has upgraded their pay and benefits now to the point that it is a very desirable department to be a part of, and that is a good thing.

So I basically just had to sign back on with HFD and attend a forty-hour refresher training course out at the academy; it consisted of a test about the rules and regulations and three training burns in the burn building—cake.

There is a lesson here for saving important documents and having them with you if you even think you might need them. I had a written letter from an HFD fire chief; it gave me permission to come back to HFD and welcomed me back to the department.

I went downtown to get my bunker gear and badge one day, and as far as I knew, everything was going great. As

I was out doing training, the new fire chief heard that some guy received his badge back. He drove all the way out to the academy to find out what was going on. I guess he was bored that day. Being the new chief, he knew nothing about my return and demanded proof. I calmly produced the signed letter from the last fire chief and all of the supporting documents processing me back into the department. This seemed to satisfy everyone, and even though he was not the chief at the time, he was bound to honor the agreement made before he came into office, as a good man should.

After he left, the senior captain in charge of me asked if I knew how close I was to being sent home without a job. I asked why would the fire chief of the fourth largest department in the nation even know about me and care enough to drive all the way across town to check it out. Neither of us had an answer, and I gave thanks to the Lord for taking care of me.

Chapter 6

Station 9

When the city has control over where you will work, instead of you being able to choose, obviously they will send you to a station that has low manpower. And if a station has low manpower, there is usually a reason guys don't want to work there. At the time, Station 9 on the C shift seemed to be one of those places. As far as runs go, the box and pumper weren't much different than most other stations inside the loop. You will make some fires, shootings, and stabbings, and you will make many nonsensical EMS calls.

Two locations made 9's box a little miserable though —2406 North Main, the Salvation Army's main location that was about four blocks away, and a known homeless hangout at 505 Hogan. These weren't the only two frequent-flyer addresses, but these were the two most notorious for 9's.

Another factor in 9's C shift having openings was the reputation of the captain. I did not know a thing about the guy, but I heard several stories upon my arrival there. He either liked or disliked you right away. By the grace of

God—and I mean that—he must have liked me because he never treated me badly while I was assigned to Station 9.

This brings me to a point I have noticed about firefighters and their complaints about captains. The C shift at the time, across the city, was known to have the worst captains. From a guy at 34's, to a notorious captain at 25's, to captains at 19's and 46's—the C shift was a who's who of captains that the guys hated. But I have noticed that on many occasions, firefighters hate captains simply because they think they themselves would do things differently and, of course, better. It is usually the nonmilitary guys who have these problems, as those of us who served usually know that you are going to serve under both poor leaders and great ones.

Your captain is not there to be your good friend and beer-drinking buddy. If that happens, fine, but there is a list of problems that can arise from that. Your captain is there to lead men, establish command and control, and maintain discipline and respect. If you have a legitimate concern, then talk to the captain in private, face-to-face. Do NOT disrespect him in front of the men, as this is not only extremely unprofessional behavior, but it will also do nothing to help your cause with him.

If you and your captain can never hammer out at least a working relationship, then you have three choices: promote yourself, transfer to another station, or wait until the captain is promoted if he is testing. Do not go around and sow seeds of dissension and contempt. This is the behavior of small, petty people who insist everything in their lives go their way. Not only is that not possible, but this is neither professional behavior nor, in my book, manly behavior. It falls under petty, junior-high immaturity, in my opinion.

Be a professional in both job performance and behavior. And yes, I am fully aware that I am expecting too much out of many people out there, but I will stand in that corner even if I am there alone.

Depressed Nation

Station 9 is on Hogan and Main Street, just a few blocks north of the skyscrapers and a few blocks east of an upscale Houston neighborhood known as the Heights, which has always been kind of a joke to me. True, it is made up of charming older houses, and it has nice trees and parks, but if you go three blocks east or north, you are on some of the worst streets in Houston. The Heights is basically an island of wealthy people in overpriced houses surrounded by an ocean of the hood with all of the crackheads, homeless, and trouble that usually is found in such places. To each his own, I guess.

On Ambulance 509 and Squad 9, we made calls to the Heights every day. Most were the normal calls for elderly falls, chest pain, or injured children, but that is not what is making me write about this area. I assume that many, if not all, of the affluent areas in Houston are very much the same, but I don't know because most of my career has been spent in the poorest areas of the city. The thing that I noticed about the Heights was that with very few exceptions, every call I made to adults and some children, the patient was on some kind of antidepressant. I can honestly say almost all of them. Most of the time, it was the young, pretty mothers who included the medications in their list of meds, and I found this interesting.

I would see a large, beautiful house with a professionally manicured lawn, a couple of Mercedes or Land Rovers (another cliche—these off-road, thoroughbred vehicles that have never been off the gravel parking lot of a soccer field) in the driveway. I would see a couple of beautiful children playing and a young, pretty, perfectly coiffed mother wearing expensive clothes—the very picture of the American dream, right? And yet almost every one of these patients was on some kind of antidepressant.

I was not the only one who noticed this because everyone at the station commented on the same thing, and we discussed it several times. The firemen came up with lots of reasons for this, but most are not PG-rated. I honestly have no answer. It could be due to a husband who ignores her physically and emotionally and works all the time, a medical system that overprescribes this type of medication, a life different from what she thought it would be, or they could be just plain old bored. It is probably a combination of all of these things.

I can say for sure that very, very few of the true medical patients that I transported in the Fifth Ward, Denver Harbor, South Park and Ship Channel areas were on mood meds, as compared to the people in the Heights who, from all outward appearances, had it made but needed antidepressants to cope with their lives.

"You da man!"

One of my more memorable runs while at 9's was a slip/fall call to a local Asian-owned corner store. We arrived on Ambulance 509 to find a man lying on the floor in front of the counter, the business owner shaking his head and standing over him.

We asked what happened and were told by the patient that he slipped on a wet spot on the floor and hit his elbow. The owner told us, "He fake fall" and "People do all the time," in a heavy Asian accent. He was probably right, but that was not up to us to decide, so we started our primary exam based on the patient's chief complaint.

While I was kneeling, checking the man out and asking questions, a lady behind us started yelling at the owner and wanting to know how much an ice cream bar was. "Yo…how much dis ice cream? YO! HOW MUCH DIS ICE

CREAM?!" She was not going to be inconvenienced by the fact that two HFD personnel with bags and a man lying on the floor were in her way. Frustrated at being ignored by the owner, she yelled louder as she stepped right between me and the patient on the floor to get to the counter.

Well, enough was enough. I stood up, got right in her face, and asked her, "Ma'am, are you not able to see that we have a situation here and that you are interfering with our work?"

She looked at me and with large hand gesticulations said, "OHHHHHH…YOU DA MAN, AND YOU IN CHARGE!!" To which, I said yes. She dropped the ice-cream bar right on the floor and shouted, "YOU DA MAN!" several times while almost running out of the store.

It was quiet again. My partner looked at me and told me that he always knew I was the man.

61 Riesner

Almost every Houston EMT who has done any time on the box near downtown knows the address 61 Riesner. This is the HPD jail off Houston Avenue, and almost all of the calls are "jailhouse chest pain." This means that someone got arrested for any number of things and suddenly thinks that claiming chest pain from a heart attack will keep them from going to jail. In reality, all this does is postpone going to jail by a few hours.

I remember one class act we made at the jail. He was claiming chest pain, of course, and had obviously been arguing with the police and giving them a hard time. He was "assisted" into the back of the cop car and decided that he would claim his chest was hurting so that he would be taken to Ben Taub Hospital.

We arrived and assisted him onto the stretcher while he was putting on a good show of how much his chest hurt and of being almost semiconscious. HPD made it very clear that they were going to meet him at the hospital and take him right to jail when cleared by the doctor.

So we kept him on oxygen and were about to shut the doors and transport him when the "patient," thinking no one but the arresting officer was looking, opened his eyes, looked at the arresting officer, shot him the finger, and went right back to his act of moaning from chest pain. Well, this sent the officer into a rage, and he started to charge the guy, but was held back by his partner.

I happened to see the flip-off myself and knew what the cop was angry about. I quickly loaded the patient, hopped in the back, and told my driver to get going. The officer made sure the patient knew that he would be waiting for him.

En route to Ben Taub, I starting gathering my patient information and taking vital signs again. I just ignored his sob story that I had heard a hundred times before from guys who can't seem to do this apparently difficult thing called "obey the law."

He asked me what I thought. I told him that I saw him flip off the cop, and then I just stared at him. Something seemed to change in him, and he was quiet the rest of the way.

I cannot express to the reader enough that there is a part of society out there that decides to not abide by the social contract that as a civilized society, keeps things from going straight to chaos when the law is not around. And then when the law catches them, they try to shift blame to the police for enforcing the law.

Unknown Problem

The ever-present "unknown problem" is a very common call we as firemen get when 911 call takers are not able to distinguish exactly what the problem is on the other end of the line. This could be due to the caller hanging up and not answering the callback, a small child being the actual caller and not relating what is happening, or maybe the caller is too stressed out or in too much pain and not mentally able to give an account of what is going on. It could be a myriad of other reasons as well, but the "unknown problem" is like Forrest Gump's box of chocolates...you never know what you are going to get.

One that sticks out in my memory was an "unknown problem" at a Dairy Queen a mile or two from Station 9. I was in charge of A509 that day, and as we got close to the scene, we saw Engine 30 and a crowd of people. *Okay, things just got a little more interesting.* We pulled up, got out, and shoved our way through the crowd, yelling at people to get out of our way. We found E30's crew on the ground, below the drive-through window, frantically placing occlusive dressings on what turned out to be five gunshot wounds to a man's chest.

The captain on the pumper looked up and asked if we were the medic unit. I said no and that we were A509 (a basic unit). I told him the call came in as an "unknown problem," and we were all they were going to get. The captain proceeded to curse fire-department procedures while we put the patient on the backboard, and then on the stretcher, and loaded him in the back.

In EMT school, we are taught the difference between staying on scene to do interventions and a load-and-go scenario in which the wounds are so severe the best thing for the patient is to be transported immediately to a trauma center and do what you can on the way. This was for sure a load-and-go.

Being a basic unit, we had no IV capabilities and therefore no way to give the patient fluid volume needed to prevent shock due to blood loss. If the reader has never been alone in the back of an ambulance with a patient who has massive trauma and is dying in front of your eyes, then I can't quite describe the combination of thoughts racing through my brain. My first thought was for an ALS (advanced life support) intercept to meet us en route to the hospital to give this guy the best chance of living, so that is what I did.

I called dispatch and told them I needed immediate ALS intercept for multiple gunshot wounds to the chest. They gave me Squad 9, which was good. I talked to Squad 9 and told them to meet on the slab in front of Station 9 because we would be going back by the station on the way to Ben Taub Hospital. I yelled at the guy driving to stop at 9's and pick up the squad. I am doing all of this while being thrown around in the back of the box while trying to get a blood pressure reading, assisting the patient with ventilations, and controlling bleeding. Plain and simply put, I needed help.

I felt us slow down and then stop; then the back doors opened up, and I was never so glad to see our two medics step into the back. I told them this came in as an unknown problem, and we simply loaded and hauled ass. Large-bore IVs were established, and we continued to Ben Taub, giving the guy every chance of survival within our capabilities.

To be honest with the reader, I don't remember if the guy eventually lived or died at Ben Taub. Just too many calls to keep them all straight, but I do know that he was still alive when we got him to the trauma room. I want to say he eventually lived through it.

How this came in as an unknown problem, I will never know, but that is life in the big city.

$10,000

Back at one of our favorite locations, 61 Riesner, we made a patient sitting in the back of a cop car; he was complaining of chest pains as he was about to be booked into the jail —surprise, surprise. It seems he was driving his Porsche 911 a little too fast and got pulled over.

We arrived to find Squad 6 already on location, their monitor hooked up, and the patient on oxygen. The paramedic decided to ride into St. Luke's Hospital with us because it turned out that this patient was a doctor with friends and connections in the Houston medical community in which we worked. The patient's vitals and heart rhythm were normal, of course. The medic could have just let us take him in, but I believe the paramedic on the squad wanted to not give any opening for this guy to complain and therefore chose to ride to the hospital with us.

While en route, we heard the usual stuff about how wrong the cops were, whom he knew and ate lunch with every week, how respected a surgeon in town he was, how he knew something was wrong, and various other drivel that drunk, self-aggrandizing rich guys say.

We arrived at St. Luke's, and I went to find a bed and set it by the door. We unloaded the doctor, transferred him to the bed from the ambulance stretcher, and took him to triage, as is the usual procedure.

After we got him admitted and to his exam room, the medic leaned over and told me to stay far away from that patient and don't say anything else to him. He told me that the "good doctor" was trouble. I, of course, asked why. Apparently, while I was getting the bed, the doctor offered the medic $10,000 to state in his report that the police were wrong and that Jim could find no presence of alcohol in the patient.

I laughed and asked him if the doctor had ten grand in cash on him right then? If not, no deal. The medic chuckled and said no; the doctor offered to write him a check. We both just laughed and shook our heads.

Sorry, Doc, but our careers, pensions, and reputations as men of honor are not for sale and sure as heck worth more than ten grand. The blood test will override any opinion we put in our report about your state of intoxication anyway, and you are not going to buy your way out of this one, as I am sure you have done in the past many times.

Street People

Working stations in the downtown area allows the fireman to interact with a special kind of human being—street people. Unless the reader volunteers at a shelter or works at a downtown, big-city ER, they have never encountered these people or given them more than a passing glance from a car window.

I do not doubt that a percentage of the homeless are mentally ill and truly need help. I also do not doubt that a certain percentage are down on their luck and have been through a series of unfortunate events, have tumbled to where they are now, and need a helping hand. But let there be no doubt that a large—very large—percentage of homeless street people seem to choose the lifestyle of a vagabond.

Some would say that is crazy. Why would anyone choose that? I would agree, but I have dealt with too many young, healthy homeless who could work, but choose instead to beg on the corners and "be free." Not all street people are the stereotypical old man who clutches a bottle of cheap red wine in a brown bag and looks like Robinson Crusoe's grandpa. And drugs are almost always part of the equation.

Street people can also be divided into other subcategories. Some are shelter dwellers who are down on their luck; they live at a shelter and may or may not have some kind of job while they are trying to get back on their feet. Then there is the true "street person" who does not shower, has not changed clothes in a long time, is drunk or high most of the time, and emits an odor that is very hard to describe.

At Station 9, we had to deal with these people regularly due to the proximity of homeless shelters in the area, the main ones being the Salvation Army at 2406 North Main Street and the Star of Hope Mission on Ruiz Street.

We were called to the shelter so many times that after a while, I started to resent the Salvation Army even though they are an outstanding private organization doing what they can. I finally had to realize that they are simply outnumbered and overwhelmed, just as we are in the EMS system.

Another fact of working in the downtown area, or any area with a large population of feral people walking around, is that you must lock the station up all the time, you cannot leave your boots on the bay floor when making a run, and you cannot leave anything of value in the bed of your pickup. One time, I forgot in the bed of my truck a sleeping cot that I had used for a camping trip; it was gone in the morning.

At most stations, guys leave their boots on the bay floor when a fire call comes in and they slip off their work boots and put on fire gear. As a result of being downtown, the homeless would come in and steal a free pair of work boots and anything else of value in the bay. We have caught the homeless wandering up into the station on many occasions. I was even sitting at the dining table upstairs when a street person came into the lounge and started mumbling about something. I quickly escorted her downstairs and let her know that upstairs was off-limits. I guess she slipped by the guy in the watch office.

We have come back from runs and found street people sitting in our chairs on the bay floor, waiting for us to return and take them to the hospital. Or they wanted us to accompany them to where they were sleeping in order to settle some argument, check on their friend, check on their pets—I have always been curious how these dogs get fed—and other things that slip my memory right now. In a nutshell, it felt as if we were under a constant barrage of calls from the street people.

Violent Way to Go

Despite my joking here and there about the homeless, I am not immune to the struggles of their plight. If anything, having face-to-face interactions with them exposed me to their situation more than almost any other job would have. I laugh at pundits on TV who think they are experts on things but have never been up close and personal with a street person, illegal alien, or junkie who has overdosed in the parking lot of some dive. Yet they tell me what I should think about such issues.

I do remember one run in particular that made my heart go out to this guy because of how it appeared he met his end. A brutal end to what was more than likely a rough life for his last several years and, most certainly, his last several moments.

Riding Engine 9, we were dispatched to an injured party lying on "the bricks" about ten thirty one night. The call came into dispatch from an anonymous caller, and we were given a very vague location near the railroad-track tunnel that goes over North Main Street just a couple of blocks from the station. So we went past the tunnel and turned right into some parking lots across from UH Downtown and started looking around. This area is part of the old railroad system from at least a century earlier, and there are many old brick loading docks and platforms dotting the area. PD arrived and helped with the search, but still we found nothing. We called dispatch for more information, and dispatch told us that they just received a call saying we were looking at the wrong group of platforms. Clearly, whoever called it in was watching us from the shadows.

We walked over to another set of brick loading docks, and, sure enough, we found a body, except this body was far beyond "injured." This body was cold, stiff, and had been very dead for several hours. His head was a beaten, bloody mess with disjointed eye sockets, teeth broken, and major blunt trauma. It was obvious to us that he was bludgeoned to death by someone wielding a hammer, pipe, or something else. PD assumed the scene since it was now a murder scene.

I have seen many, many dead people from all kinds of causes and have felt sorry for most, not sorry for some, and indifferent to others. But I felt sorry for this homeless guy who stood at the wrong end of a violent person's path. But, then again, I don't know the story. Maybe this victim was actually the attacker, and the person who killed him acted in self-defense and then anger. It's possible, but the amount of damage to the guy looked as if it was more than just a blow to stop someone from attacking. This looked personal. One thing I knew for sure was that, no matter the story, this was an unpleasant death. To be honest, I am not sure I have seen a pleasant death.

505 Hogan

Anyone who worked at 9's a few years ago knows this address. I have heard that this house was actually torn down recently, and if that is true, then the city did that area a huge favor. This was an old, rickety house that had been occupied by multiple street people for years, and it was the address given in EMS calls daily. There was never a time that I went there that there were not at least a dozen people in the house, spread out in every room, among the filth and debris. As we made calls, we could hear people moving around up in the attic above us, doing who knows what.

Drug calls, beatings, and psych calls—the usual stuff —were all the order of the day at 505 Hogan Street, and the smell of the place was enough to make you want to shower after coming out of there.

The Woods

Most cities I have been to have little "islands" of trees in between freeway interchanges, under overpasses, and at other places like that. Some in Houston can be an acre or two in size, and if they are that big and your city has a homeless population, you can bet there are street people camped out in there. You may not see them, but they are there. There was a section just like that where Hogan crossed over Interstate 45, just north of downtown Houston. One call there I will never forget.

We were flagged down by a guy who led us for a few yards on a worn path to a tarp-covered, plywood-crate shelter hidden by the thick trees. His buddy was sick and could not move. We investigated and found a very sick male wrapped in a filthy sleeping bag and covered with human excrement. Not only was he covered in it, but it was all over the ground around him and very hard not to step in while trying to attend to this guy.

We finally got him on the stretcher, and we all had to decontaminate the bottoms of our boots, inspect each other to make sure no one had any on their uniforms, and try not to throw up for the next hour while the smell slowly left our nostrils. Good times indeed.

Happy New Year

One particular New Year's Eve while I was assigned to Station 9 stands out in my memory because of the pure anger and sadness that the situation caused in me. I was on A509 and dispatched to an MVA (motor vehicle accident) on the outbound lane of Highway 59 North. We arrived to find several police cars, Engine 19, Ladder 19, and Medic 19, all on the scene of a devastating wreck.

A drunk driver in a sedan got on the off-ramp to 59 and started going against traffic until he hit head-on a blue minivan being driven by a man trying to get home after working late on New Year's Eve. The van was destroyed, the driver instantly killed, and the ladder truck was still trying to extricate the body with their hydraulic tools.

I found out the driver was already in the medic unit, so I went over to see if I could be of any assistance. The guy driving the box was an academy classmate of mine, and he filled me in on what was going on and informed me that although the innocent man was killed, the drunk was barely injured and walking around at the scene.

I have heard several theories on why the drunks seem to avoid injury, and the prevailing one is that they don't tense up at the moment of impact; they are more "loose" when they are restrained by the seat belt and airbag. I don't know if this is true or false, but I have seen many drunks appear to be fine or only slightly injured at accidents with major damage.

This particular drunk was on the backboard in C-spine immobilization, passed out on the stretcher. While I was talking to my buddy, the drunk moaned and slurred something. My friend leaned over him and said, "Happy New Year, you killed a man tonight." The drunk slurred something else and passed back out.

The word "anger" was not sufficient to describe what I felt about this loser. Because of him, some family members were getting the worst phone call of their lives that night, and here we were, having to take care of this piece of work.

I don't know what happened to the drunk driver, but I hope that he is still in jail today and that some slick-talking lawyer did not get him a reduced sentence somehow.

Roaches, Rodents, and Such

I would think that every firefighter out there has stories about these types of critters, and mine come from all across the city. So I will just bunch them all together, except for the fiery rat that I covered earlier.

I have made two patients with roaches that have crawled into their ear canals while sleeping. I can tell you that they were both freaked out to the extreme, which is understandable. One guy was yelling that he could feel and hear the roach kicking around in his ear. He had to be held down while the paramedics solved this problem.

The reader may be wondering how exactly you solve this problem. It is actually fairly simple. You pour alcohol into the ear canal to kill the roach and then reach in with a pair of forceps and pull it out. I have to say that the thought of a roach in my ear terrifies me.

I have made calls to filthy homes that were so infested with roaches we had to go back to the truck and put on our fire helmets and bunker coats with the collars turned up to keep the roaches from dropping down our shirts while putting a patient on a backboard—not kidding.

Another pest that firefighters deal with on a pretty regular basis is the rat, at least if your territory is made up of older houses or in parts of the city that have a lot of abandoned houses.

I remember one of my first fires as a rookie at 34's. I was next to the senior captain while helping stretch out some hose in the front lawn of an older house that was fully involved with fire. I looked up on the roof above the front porch and saw dozens of rats trying to escape the fire below. So many, in fact, that it kind of caught me off guard.

The captain yelled at me to stop looking around and to get back to work. He later joked at the station that the rookie likes to look at rats instead of fighting fire.

One very large fire at a plant nursery, we were wetting down some outbuildings made of corrugated tin, and as one of the metal roofs that had collapsed was lifted, there was a soaking-wet, large opossum underneath. I saw him at the same time the crew on the next hand line did, and I heard the guy on the nozzle yell, "Look at that big effing rat!" I just laughed and let him keep thinking he saw a rat the size of a cat that day.

Chapter 7

Station 77

Because Station 9 was an administrative assignment, I was allowed to put in for a transfer when the next transfer posting became open. My best friend was assigned to Station 77, which is on the west side of Houston and would cut down on my drive time by about twenty-five minutes. So I put in for 77 A shift and was able to get it.

At the time, 77's box was much slower, and it also had a ladder truck and a pumper, which meant that I would have more rotation time to ride a fire truck and go back to putting the wet stuff on the red stuff. After Hurricane Katrina, though, the ambulance at Station 77 became a completely different animal, as did many others across the city, almost doubling in call volume from about eight to ten calls a day to thirteen to fifteen. Yes, many ambulances make eighteen every day, but any fireman will tell you that the only count that really matters is how many calls you make after midnight. After Katrina, 77's was good for at least three runs after midnight every night. It wasn't like that before.

Why? Because thousands of Katrina refugees from New Orleans were put in thousands of apartments in District 5, and let me tell you, dear reader, they like to dial 911. Some people got offended by the term "refugee." Well, if you are seeking refuge from a storm and a city that has ceased to function, are you not a refugee?

Before Katrina, though, many of 77's calls came from a group of apartments on Pittner Street; they were affectionately referred to as Pittner Pitts. It is a huge apartment complex that is, for all practical purposes, a colony of people from Mexico and Central America.

Another large portion of our calls at 77's was to the assisted living/retirement community directly across from our station. For obvious reasons, this address was a common number on our dispatches. I remember one particular day when Ladder 77 was asked to come demonstrate proper fire-extinguisher technique to a gathering of these residents in their dining hall.

Save My Dog

Let me preface this by saying that I have a dog, and I like my dog and would never want to see Petey die in a fire or be hurt in any way. But I live in the REAL WORLD. And here in the real world, a human life and a dog's life are not equal.

So there we were, in front of several dozen elderly residents, talking about fire safety, and at the end of the presentation, we were taking questions. After a few questions, one lady stood up and asked the senior captain if we would save her dog at all costs in case of a fire.

The captain explained to her that, of course, we would do everything we could to find and save her dog, unless conditions became so bad that a firefighter might die in the course of looking for her dog.

This answer was not good enough for her because she stated with an air of disbelief that her dog was her "child."

I asked the captain if I could answer her, and I was given permission. In front of all of these senior citizens, I asked her, "Ma'am, if someone was pointing a cocked, loaded .357 Magnum handgun at your dog and about to pull the trigger, would you jump in front of the gun and take the bullet for your pet?"

"Well...no," she answered.

"Well, I would for my kids without even thinking about it. Please don't compare your pet to children because that puts your dog on the same level as my children. For people, we are going to risk our lives to save them, but a pet's life is not worth the risk of making two young boys fatherless and a wife a widow."

We moved on to the next question.

Potato Babies

In my years in the EMS system, I have come extremely close to delivering several babies, but have actually delivered only one in the field. I have taken many, many pregnant women by ambulance to the hospital by picking them up in front of their houses, suitcases in hand and vehicles in the driveway.

You know, we are the EMERGENCY taxi service. I have two sons, and when my wife went into labor on both occasions, I put her into the car and drove her to the hospital. I did not dial 911.

"Potato baby" has nothing to do with the shape or appearance of the child, and everything to do with what I learned in EMT school. We were taught to wrap a newborn in a blanket and then wrap aluminum foil around the blanket to keep them warm. The nurses in the ER would joke that they looked like baked potatoes all wrapped in foil.

My partner and I arrived at an apartment one day for an OB (obstetrics) call. We made it upstairs to find not a single person who spoke English, and we finally were directed to the back bedroom where a woman was sitting on the floor against the wall, the baby's head crowning and about to come out.

I broke open the OB kit and grabbed trauma dressings while my partner bent down to catch the baby that was on his way. About thirty seconds later, he held the baby while I clamped the cord and cut it. I then proceeded to administer an Apgar test and wrap the baby in the aforementioned potato costume. He was alert and healthy. About that time, Medic 49 arrived on scene. The baby and mother were fine, so we were going to transport them in the basic ambulance because there was no need for advanced protocols.

Being a little bit frustrated that less than a minute after we came through the door we were holding a newborn, I asked the medic why the mother would wait so long to call. If she was just suddenly surprised and had a two-minute labor and birthing process, then she set a speed record. In other words, she was in labor with plenty of time and people to take her to the hospital, so why did she wait until the baby was almost born to call EMS? She could have gone to the hospital a few hours earlier.

The medic said that in his experience, this was very common. This way, they can have their babies delivered by medical professionals with emergency equipment, and there is no major hospital bill. There will be an ambulance bill for the transport, but good luck on collecting that money.

The Munchies

I made a car wreck one day on A77. A lady was hit from behind by a large truck while she was leaving a Subway sandwich shop. I arrived to find two bystanders talking to the lady and helping her as best they could.

She had significant damage to the rear of her vehicle and complained of neck pain. So we started spinal immobilization by holding her C-spine and putting a neck collar on her. We then transferred her to a backboard, taped her down, and began to load her into the ambulance for transport.

While we were rolling her on the stretcher to the ambulance doors, one of the bystanders stopped us and said, "Ma'am, can we have those subs on your front seat?"

She responded, "Oh my gosh… Fine, take them."

The man looked at his buddy standing by the car and nodded. His friend then, with great satisfaction, reached into the smashed car and grabbed two foot-long subs.

I just laughed.

Selfish

I remember a call during which my captain made me go outside because of how angry I became at the mother of a teenage patient. I was on Engine 77, and we made a call to an asthma patient at some apartments off Emnora Drive. We got up to the scene and entered to find a teenage girl in clear respiratory distress in an apartment full of cigarette smoke.

I asked the mother to please put out her cigarette, and she asked why. I said—and, I admit, in an "I'm fed up with stupid people" voice—that we were using pure oxygen, that her daughter was having an asthma attack, and that she shouldn't be smoking around her asthmatic daughter in the first place.

Well, this selfish idiot did not like someone calling her out. She barked back at me, "Who do you think you are?"

I replied, "A professional EMT who knows a few things about patients who are having difficulty breathing."

Our voices were getting louder, and my captain told me to go outside and direct the medic unit to the correct apartment. It was the right call, as I was probably pretty close to really getting into trouble with this sorry excuse for a parent. A parent who has an asthmatic daughter, whom I assume she loves, but is too selfish to simply go outside to smoke her precious cigarette.

Excuses

Before the days of Depressed Nation and people taking mood meds with their morning coffee, the American population turned to good old-fashioned alcohol to numb their worries. Of course, there are still holdouts who practice the old ways, and one morning I was fortunate enough not only to meet one and transport her, but as an added bonus, to make her angry by not accepting her excuses.

Around ten in the morning, we made an "alcohol-related problem," according to the dispatcher. We arrived on the scene to find a lady in her fifties in a mildly drunken state and smelling of liquor. She told us she did not feel good and wanted to go to the hospital. So we loaded her up.

During the interview, I think she could tell that I was not very sympathetic to her condition, so she said to me, "It's a disease, you know…like cancer."

I looked up from my report and asked what was. She said alcoholism, and this was her mistake. I told her flatly, "No. It is not like cancer. I transport innocent cancer patients almost daily. People *choose* to start drinking. People *choose* to have one more drink and then another. People *choose* to put effort into going to the liquor store to buy another bottle. I agree that you have a problem that is out of your control now, but it is a problem you created by thousands of poor choices. Women don't go to the breast-cancer store and *choose* to have cancer, so you don't get to excuse yourself by comparing your condition to cancer."

Her eyes shot daggers at me, and I stared right back at her. This is the problem with America today. It is ALWAYS someone or something else's fault when, in fact, most miserable conditions are a product of poor choices that have not been owned up to and corrected.

She didn't say another word to me, and I just completed my record on the way to the hospital. I knew she was probably going to file a complaint about me, but to her credit, I never heard anything. Maybe, just maybe, she heard what I said.

Bubbles in the Blood

On Engine 77 one night, we were called to a shooting at a gas station down the road from the station on Beltway 8. We arrived to find police cars everywhere, and as we walked in, we were told to be careful of the bloody sneaker prints that were leading from behind the counter, all the way outside.

Behind the counter, we found a store clerk lying on his stomach on the ground, his head facing to his right. Surrounding his head was a very large and very thick pool of blood, and it was obvious that the gunshot was probably somewhere to the face area. The left side of his face was in the middle of the blood puddle, with one nostril covered and one still above the level of the blood. With his labored breathing, this poor fellow was blowing bubbles in the pool of blood, out of the one nostril that was covered. It never ceases to amaze me that small details like that can stick out in your memory.

We loaded this victim as quickly as possible and tried to give him every chance to live, but the damage was too great; he did not survive.

From then on, I thought about that poor guy every time I passed that gas station. I stopped to get fuel there a couple of months after this, and I noticed that the owners had installed a wall of bulletproof glass around the counter.

Choice?

One call on E77 was to an assault by a boyfriend with a baseball bat to the abdomen of his pregnant girlfriend. Obviously, this guy was trying to get rid of the baby in a very brutal fashion. We arrived and immediately rushed the victim to the hospital for care. The boyfriend was charged with attempted murder of both the mother and fetus.

I found these charges completely correct, but interesting in another way. We rushed over to the scene with lights and sirens and started emergency care to save the fetus and mother. The boyfriend was arrested and charged with multiple felonies. We transported the mother and child with lights and sirens to the emergency room and gave all possible care to help the baby live, which it did.

So what if the next week the mother decides she no longer wants the baby and walks down to the abortion clinic and kills the child? One week the baby is a citizen worthy of all emergency care and attempted murder charges, and the next the mother can just end the baby's life? What changed?

Do not try telling me that it is not really a child until he/she is born. I have made several calls for miscarriages over the years, and I even had to fish a fetus out of a toilet after the mother thought she needed to have a bowel movement. This was not a pleasant thing to do, and let me assure you that those babies were not just a mass of tissue. They had little toes, fingers, eyes, and ears and were simply unborn children.

No Room

On A77 one night we made a call to some apartments on Beltway 8 for a laceration. It was a laceration, for sure, but somewhat more serious than just your normal cut that needed a few stitches. There was blood all over the apartment from a guy who either got thrown or fell through a large window—I let the cops figure that out. He had several severe cuts but one very deep laceration on his forearm with arterial bleeding that was squirting blood.

We immediately got him in the ambulance and started for the nearest ER while I was in the back by myself trying to stop blood flow and get a set of vitals. We were just a few blocks from the hospital when we stopped in the middle of the feeder road for a reason not known to me. I looked out the little window on the side door and could see the hospital just down the street. I was about to yell when we took off again at a high rate of speed.

After getting the patient to the ER and turned over to the ER staff, I asked my driver why we stopped. My driver told me that a guy jumped out in front of the ambulance and flagged us down. We stopped, and the guy was yelling about his friend being shot. My driver asked if he called 911, and the guy said yes and asked if we were that ambulance. Brian said no; we had a guy in the back already bleeding all over the place, and we were rushing him to the ER.

At that point, my driver saw the red lights from another ambulance come around the corner, heading in our direction. He confirmed that the next station's ambulance was indeed the ambulance assigned to the guy in the street. Right when I was about to lose patience in the back and start yelling, he hit the gas again and got our patient to the ER.

Ship Fire

One time, I was sent to fill in at Station 26, which is all the way across town from Station 77. I had worked at 26's before, so I wasn't too unfamiliar with the station and territory.

After midnight that night, we were sent on a two-alarm fire at the Houston Ship Channel. A cargo ship was burning from down in the hold, and ship crews had not been able to get it under control.

We arrived to see a huge cargo ship with black smoke pouring out of it, and we made our way down the dock to command for assignment. We were assigned to go down into the hold and relieve another crew that was already down there with a hand line.

The seat of the fire was deep in the middle of hundreds of large wooden boxes in the hold, so our water was not really getting to the source. The decision was made to use the crane to lift out the heavy wood crates until the source of the fire could be determined and doused.

Now, being down there with the hose line in hot, smoky conditions was not fun, but when I saw what the ship crew was tasked to do, I was okay with my assignment. These poor guys, from who knows what country, were riding the crane cable down to the top of the stack of boxes, attaching the crates to the cables, and riding the boxes back up, all without any protective gear that I could see. No air pack, no bunker gear, not even a bandanna…and they were right in the middle of the worst part of the smoke and heat going up from the hold into the night air through the large top doors. I could not help but feel sorry for them.

"Murder Cleaners"

In the movies about the Mafia or in hitmen-related movies, there is usually a group of people who show up after the hit or shoot-out and clean up the crime scene to make it look as though nothing ever happened. One day on A77, I found out that such people actually exist…kind of.

We were called to a motel on Highway 290 on a "sick call" for a patient in one of the hotel rooms. We arrived to find the hotel manager and a police officer standing outside a room and shaking their heads. There was also a terrible smell coming from the room. We walked in to find the patient sitting on the end of the bed, and my partner and I almost vomited on the spot. The "patient" had stomach problems and had let loose with diarrhea all over the room. The carpet, bed, bathroom floor…everywhere. In multiple spots for multiple days too.

We loaded him up while trying not to gag, and all the way out, I asked the manager what on earth could they do with the room besides burn it? He said they had "murder cleaners" whom they called to come and clean up rooms in which people were shot or committed suicide. Both obviously make a tremendous mess, but these industrial, non-Mafia-related cleaning agencies specialize in cleaning even scenes like that one. He did admit that the mattress would probably have to be replaced.

Field Amputation

Interstate 10 runs right through the middle of Houston and, of course, is a major source of not only traffic jams during all times of the day, but also auto accidents. There are a few wrecks, out of the seemingly hundreds, that stand out in my memory. One involving a lady and her F-150 pickup is set in my memory, not because of the number of victims or the absolute carnage across the freeway, but rather because what we did treating the victim was not a normal day's work.

It seemed that this woman had been driving down the freeway with her windows down, her left arm resting on the bottom of the window opening. A sudden stop ahead of her caused her to swerve with enough momentum to flip her truck onto the driver's side and slide to a stop. The problem was that her arm was outside of the truck window during the wreck, between the road and the top of the door. The results were that the arm was connected by a very small piece of skin and that was about it when we arrived on scene.

The truck was resting on the driver's side, and the woman was crumpled up against the door and the ground; her broken, almost-amputated-at-the-elbow arm was inside the window, and the rest of her arm was outside. MD3 (medical director number three, a supervising trauma doctor, one of several who responds to calls around the city) happened to arrive on the scene, and he saw that to free the woman, we were about to use air bags to lift the vehicle and cribbing to stabilize it while tenderly extricating her through the front windshield. This process takes time.

He inspected the arm and decided to do what we all were thinking. He pulled out his trauma shears and snipped the last strands of flesh barely holding the arm together. Having done this, we were able to simply pick up her arm, wrap it up with cold packs, and more quickly get her out of the truck, loaded into the ambulance, and on her way.

"Prepare for a Lawsuit"

A few blocks away from Station 77 is a very large nursing home that was the location of many calls for cardiac arrests because the majority of patients in the facility are old and nearing the end of their lives. One such call stands out in my memory because of what was said by a family member after the ninety-two-year-old patient passed away.

We made the scene to find the patient in her bed, pulseless and not breathing. The amount of time the patient was down was unknown because the last time the patient was seen alive was at least a few hours earlier. So, following protocols, we started CPR (plan A in HFD language).

Now, putting a plan A into effect on a ninety-two-year-old patient with unknown downtime is always a kind of "why" moment to every EMT. I know it sounds cold and/or morbid to say, but at ninety-two years of age, maybe it is just your time to go, and the very invasive procedures that we do during a plan A may or may not be effective. Even if they are successful at bringing the patient back, it is not the same as the person simply waking up and everything normal. Chances are the patient at that age is never the same after that and simply lives a few more months as an unresponsive patient racking up massive medical bills. But that decision is made by a supervisor, and until they arrive on the scene, we initiate CPR.

After about ten minutes of working on this patient, the supervisor showed up on the scene, and after gathering all of the details, he decided to "call" (pronounce dead) the patient. It was absolutely the correct call.

I was at the nursing desk, getting information for my report, when the charge nurse called the family of the woman to give them the bad news. I heard her say who she was and that the lady had unfortunately passed away. Then I saw her look at the phone and calmly hang it up. I looked at her, she looked at me, and I asked what was said that made her hang up the phone so oddly. She said that the family member simply said, "Prepare for a lawsuit," and hung up on her.

Really? That is the first thing to come out of the guy's mouth? I asked the nurse if they gave a guarantee that patients would never pass away once admitted to their facility. She smiled and said that lawsuits were common; that is why they have a legal department.

It's my guess that lawsuits are also part of why these facilities cost so much.

"Good Thing Y'All Didn't Drop Me"

This call reminded me of a time I transported to the hospital a lady who wasn't feeling well. As I was lifting her out of the back of the ambulance, one wheel on the stretcher got caught on the step bumper that is behind the ambulance. This caused the stretcher to start to tip over slightly. My partner arrived just in time to grab it and help me to keep from spilling the patient onto the ground.

I apologized for the scare, and as we were wheeling her in, she stated, "Good thing y'all didn't drop me. I would have had your job."

I stopped the stretcher, looked at her, and asked, "Have I been polite and respectful to you this entire call? Have I taken good care of you and answered all of your questions?"

She answered yes.

I then said, "I am a father of two little boys, and you would want me to get fired for an accident and have their father lose his job? Why would you think like that?"

She said nothing—neither did I—for the rest of the call.

First Official Complaint

The first time I had a citizen officially file a complaint against me happened on a run to an office building. We arrived and found no patient to be seen and a receptionist talking on the phone at the front desk. She hung up the phone, and I asked if anyone had called 911.

She calmly said the patient was a coworker and was in the restroom. I asked her what happened. She said her coworker threw up, and she, the receptionist, dialed 911. She called 911 immediately without even asking the coworker or asking a single question to find out what was going on.

I asked her, "You called 911 simply because someone vomited?" Yes, there was probably more than a hint of frustration in my voice.

She got up, walked around the desk, looked at my name tag, and wrote it down.

We then proceeded to interview the patient. She stated that she neither called nor asked someone to call 911. She felt she probably had a touch of the flu and wanted to go home.

About a week later, I was called to the chief's office at Station 5. He showed me the letter and asked what happened. I told him what happened and what I said. He shook his head, told me that he had to document it in my file, wadded the complaint up, and basketball-shot it into the trash basket. It pays to have a good chief.

$40 Bra

A very routine motor-vehicle accident consists of a patient with moderate-to-severe damage to their car and no visible signs of obvious trauma to the patient. They will usually complain of neck, shoulder, or chest pain where the seat belt caught them, but to rule out internal injuries, they need to be transported to the hospital. Our protocols stated that any patient complaining of neck or back pain, secondary to an MVA, must be put in spinal immobilization with a neck collar and on a backboard. This is to limit as much as possible the movement of the spine and neck in order to prevent making any injuries worse. I cannot begin to tell you how many patients over the years I have strapped to a backboard in a C-collar and transported to the hospital years.

One routine call stands out in my memory because of the comment made by the patient when the doctor informed her in the trauma room that he needed to cut away her clothing in order to do a proper exam for any injuries. This is standard procedure because the patient is immobilized and cannot move; therefore, their clothing cannot be removed by normal means.

After he let her know that he had to cut her shirt away to examine injuries on her chest, she said okay and did not put up much of a fuss. He then told her that he needed to cut the straps of her bra as well. To this, she opened her eyes wider and said, "Not my bra! It cost me FO'TY DOLLAHS!."

Crepitus

When bones rub and grind against each other, it produces a condition known as crepitus. In the case of fractures, crepitus can be heard, for sure, but in my experience, it is more often felt when moving or examining a patient. It is not pleasant, and no matter how many times you have felt it, every time is still a little unnerving.

The absolute worst case of bones grating on bones I ever experienced was on a fifteen-year-old girl who was hit by a truck while walking down the road. It was a difficult call then, and it is still uncomfortable to think about it all these years later.

I was on A77 with another EMT from my station, and we got called to an "auto-ped" (automobile-pedestrian accident) over towards Station 5. We were first on the scene and arrived to find a teenage boy looking as if he was in a daze, standing over the crumpled body of a teenage girl. I was the first person to the patient, and I asked him what happened. Through tears, he stated that they were walking down the shoulder of the road when she suddenly was hit by a black truck. The truck stopped for a second and then left the scene.

My partner held her C-spine, and we rolled her over as carefully as we could to assess vital signs. While moving her, it felt as if we were rolling over a bag of gravel. It was sickening to think about the trauma that was inflicted on this poor girl's body. It seemed as if every bone in her body were busted and in pieces, including her neck and cranium. No breath sounds, no heartbeat…no life left in her at all.

Supervisor 50 arrived on scene about that time and determined what we already knew—she was DOA. I was on my knees on the street, attending to her, and I just sat back on my butt, my arms on my knees and my head down, for a couple of minutes. My partner was young and unmarried then, but he knew I had a son around her age. He simply asked if I was okay. I was honest with him. I told him that this call hit me hard, but I would be okay. He agreed.

We learned from a lady who witnessed the accident that the couple were simply walking down the neighborhood road to the local Quickie-Mart, and a black Chevy truck going way beyond the speed limit veered over and struck the girl. The woman said that the "poor child" must have flown forty feet down the road.

Firemen see and deal with things that can't be forgotten, and although this was nowhere near the bloodiest or most carnage-filled scene I had ever made, I will never forget the despair I felt while turning her body over and knowing from what we saw and felt from the inside of her that she was gone and didn't stand a chance.

Hurricane Rita

Hurricane Rita was the "great storm" that never hit. At least not in the manner we are used to hurricanes wreaking havoc. Instead, the havoc from Rita came in the form of a botched mass evacuation of the city of Houston and surrounding areas. I worked on A77 during this failed evacuation, and let me tell you from an eyewitness who was called all over the city that day…it was a complete mess.

The roads were in complete gridlock, and trying to respond to some calls was an exercise in futility. I clearly remember going on a call on I-10 westbound; it took thirty or more minutes to get to the interchange of Beltway 8 and I-10. We came to a stop, stared at the absolute ocean of cars below us, and called dispatch to let them know that we simply did not know if we could make the location. Dispatch called back and simply said, "Ambulance 77, do the best you can."

We were getting calls to the "green Chevy Suburban in front of Lowes on I-10." No address, no other details, and, quite honestly, no way to get to the car even if we knew exactly where it was. The road system in Houston was practically a parking lot. Eventually, automobiles started running out of gas and clogging up the roads even more. People tried to push them off the road but with not much success.

Nursing homes were evacuated and elderly people, who were barely alive to begin with, did not respond well to sitting for hours in traffic. I led a convoy of three ambulances to Spring Branch Hospital with CPR in progress in all three at the same time. The ER was not too excited to see us.

It was a long, difficult shift, but there was one call in the midst of the chaos that I did appreciate. We received a sick call to a gas station not too far away from the fire station. We had to go in the opposite direction on several streets to get there, and we found utter chaos in the station's parking lot. People were EVERYWHERE. Stranded cars with people in them, people strolling around, people waiting in line for the gas pumps…people everywhere.

I was driving, and my partner and I agreed that I should stay with the box while he went inside to ask who had called 911. The normal rules of society seemed to be stretched to their thinnest right at that moment. While watching the bedlam around me, I heard the sound of a motor and looked to my right. A guy on a four-wheeler was riding down the bayou; he took a right and zipped in and out of traffic to get to the gas station. He had on rubber boots and a military boonie hat. I continued to watch him calmly ride right up to the front door, hop off his ATV, and stroll inside. By this time, I was amused by him.

A few minutes later, I saw him come out with two twenty-four-packs of Busch beer, climb back on his ATV, weave in and out of traffic back to the bayou, and start heading home, I assume. I loved it. No panic, no worries—he just needed to go on a beer run, so he used the best possible solution to achieve his goal.

My partner returned and said he couldn't find any patient; we left the scene.

Chapter 8

On to Rescue

Since my time as a rookie, I had wanted to be a member of Technical Rescue. In our house, we had two main activities, outside of mountain biking—diving in the river and rock climbing. I constructed a large 360-degree bouldering wall at our Canyon Lake home, and some of my best memories are climbing on that wall with my little guys. Our vacations were climbing/hiking vacations, and being "on rope" is still today one of my favorite places to be. Doing high-angle rescue just seemed to be where I thought I would spend the rest of my career.

So I applied to the rescue class and was accepted. I could not wait to ride the rescue truck and get away from doing my ambulance rotations, but I soon learned that ropes were only a small part of being in rescue. One had to be trained to the technician level in seven disciplines—high-angle rescue, structural collapse, extrication, confined-space rescue, below-grade (trench-collapse) rescue, elevator rescue, and swift-water rescue.

My strong points were in high-angle rescue due to the crossover with climbing-rope techniques and in swift-water rescue due to the fact that I was in the Comal or Guadalupe Rivers almost every day off—still am. I was also swift-water trained by New Braunfels FD, which, I would argue, gets the most actual swift-water rescue experience in the state.

I'm not quite sure how to best approach describing the people I worked with in rescue, other than to say that most were some of the most professional, encouraging guys I have ever worked with but many were some of the most petty and backbiting people that would be jealous if you made a big call and they didn't. They were friendly and easygoing around you, and then criticized you to others behind your back. I saw them do it to other people, and I heard them do it to me. I never before or since have experienced as much of this behavior as I witnessed with the rescue team.

Overall, I would rate my three years on the rescue truck as a positive. I am glad I had the experience and was able to do the type of specialty work being a "rescue man" entails. There is no way I can remember all of the wrecks and fires I made in rescue, but some of the runs that stick out in my memory follow.

High IQ

Only one time in my career did I have to use a chain saw to cut a tree away from a car wreck before we could use the extrication tools. A fellow in a sports car took a curve in Memorial Park way too fast, lost control, and slid off the road. It probably would not have been a big deal but for the fact his car T-boned a large, standing, dead pine tree with enough force to bring the tree down right on top of his car, across the roof over the front seats. The tree completely crushed the roof of his car and him along with it.

When we jumped off the truck and scrambled down the embankment to see exactly what we would need, we were all taken aback a little to realize that a chain saw was the first tool needed. So we cut the tree into sections and removed it; then we used extrication tools to cut the roof off the car to get the body out. I remember picking up tools to take back them to the truck and noticing his license plate—HI IQ.

Tour Bus

An extremely popular Tejano singer had a bus crash on the 610 Loop, right before it crossed over Highway 59 on the west side of town. He flew out of the windshield and landed about ten feet before a drop-off of more than thirty feet to the highway below.

When we arrived, the bus was on its side, and we had to stabilize it using hydraulic shoring so that another guy and I could go inside the bus and look for more victims.

It was unclear at the scene exactly how many people were in the tour bus at the time of the accident.

We didn't find any other bodies in the bus, which is always a good thing, but the thing I remember most as we half-crawled through piles of cowboy hats, Wrangler jeans, guitars, and boxes was how many pairs of very expensive Lucchese boots were in the pile. I remember telling my partner that this guy had good taste in boots. It's funny the things you remember about certain calls years later.

Downtown Train

Houston decided to put in electric trains downtown to hopefully aid in relieving traffic congestion. When this took place, I was at Station 9, which is just a few blocks north of downtown, and we made many auto-train wrecks during that time. The main culprit seemed to be a combination of there being train tracks where none had been before and the fact that electric trains are silent. I suppose people rely on hearing a train coming as much as seeing it.

While in rescue, we went to the metro train headquarters and did some classes on how exactly to lift one of these heavy engines if a person is trapped underneath. It was a topic of much discussion because the trains had very little ground clearance, which made rescues more difficult and required employing different tactics.

In fact, the employees at the train department told us that they thought we would probably never need to lift a train engine because the low clearance would sweep a body out of the way, not run over it. They were wrong. The second field amputation I was a part of was a pedestrian under one of the trains downtown.

I happened to be driving the truck that evening when the call came in. We arrived to find a lady under the front of the train. As I started to unload the heavy-lift airbags, as well as various pieces of equipment that are used to lift a major vehicle, I was told that it looked as if we could probably first try to hold her C-spine and try to gently pull her from under the front of the train. This would be much faster for the patient and much safer for the patient and rescuer. A stable train on its tracks is much safer than a lifted train resting on airbags and cribbing. So that is what we started to do.

As we began to extricate her, we noticed that there was resistance to pulling her out, which meant that part of her was more than likely tangled up with the train in some spot we couldn't see. Using our big lights, we illuminated the space under the train as well as we could and still could not see what was keeping her from being pulled out.

So one of the guys crawled on his belly as far under as he could and discovered that one of her feet was separated from the lower leg at the ankle, but still attached by just a slight bit of tissue. The resistance was coming from a lag bolt that hung down from the train; it was jammed into the ankle bones. When we tried to pull her out, the bolt anchored in her skin and ligaments.

MD3 was again on the scene, and he made the decision to complete the amputation using trauma shears. So one of our guys slid under the train and cut the remaining tissue connecting her leg to her ankle. We then removed her from under the train while the rescuer underneath pulled her foot from the lag bolt. The patient and body part were transported together to the ER. Field amputation number two for me.

"Learn How to Drive"

One of my funnier memories in rescue came late at night after a fire. Our driver was having trouble backing the rescue truck down a dark, narrow neighborhood road. The rescue truck at Station 11 is a tractor trailer very similar to what a beer or soft-drink truck looks like, roll-up doors and all. Anyone who needed to drive the truck had to get a Class A driver's license.

We were finished with a fire call on a street just a few blocks down from the station, and the only way to get out was to back the truck about five blocks, with cars parked on both sides of the narrow street, and then turn on TC Jester Avenue. It was way after midnight, the streets were narrow and poorly lit, and there was a deep ditch on both sides of the road. So, to be honest, it was not the best situation.

Using flashlights and radios, we slowly crept backward down the street until we hit the wide avenue onto which the driver could cut the wheel and turn around. As he started to execute the maneuver, however, the cars parked on the narrow street got within inches of the front bumper of the truck, and we kept jackknifing. This made our driver stop, go forward a few feet, cut the wheels, and reverse again… repeat…a ten-point turn instead of a three-point turn.

I was in the middle of the street with another guy, and we saw a pair of headlights coming. So we flashed our lights and made a motion for the car to stop, as the trailer was halfway into the street. The car was a loud Ford Mustang that had obviously been souped up to be even faster. There were two young guys in the car; they stopped and were patient…at first.

Our driver had to repeatedly back up and pull forward, all the while preventing the Mustang from proceeding. The driver of the Mustang revved its engine over and over, wanting to get by us. After three or four more tries, I radioed to our driver to hold up and let the car get on its way. So the truck pulled forward again, and I motioned for the Mustang to come on and pass.

The car pulled up right behind the fire truck and stopped. The passenger leaned out of the window, gave us the middle finger, and yelled, "Learn how to drive, you bitch!" The Mustang then burned rubber while taking off and disappeared into the night.

My partner and I just laughed. A few tries later, our driver got turned around, and we went back to the station.

Crane Collapse

It has been difficult to write about several of these calls, if I am to be completely honest, and this next call is no different. The destruction to the human bodies my partner and I were tasked to deal with was so complete that it would be difficult to describe properly with words. I, and every firefighter, have seen humans burned to a crisp, mangled in car wrecks, drowned and eaten by crabs and crawfish, and murdered or self-terminated in more ways than most people can imagine. But the poor guys crushed by one of the largest cranes in North America were the most destroyed humans I have ever encountered, no contest.

We were dispatched to a major refinery at which, according to initial reports, a huge crane had tipped over and caused massive damage to the surrounding buildings and structures. When we arrived on scene, we drove around the collapsed crane to park. This allowed us to survey the extent of the damage. The enormity of the crane became apparent; anywhere the steel arms and support structure of the crane landed, there was a massive crater in the asphalt, and whatever happened to be in the way was crushed. We learned later that this was one of North America's top-five largest cranes. It had collapsed onto multiple buildings and storage sheds in about a 100-yard radius. The collapse zone was a total disaster and a confusing mess. The plant management had been trying to account for everyone on shift that day, and there were still four employees unaccounted for.

My partner and I were assigned a sector that would make up the nine- to twelve-o'clock section of the collapse zone, if you consider the top of the collapsed crane twelve o'clock. We were told that two men were missing from that general area.

It did not take us long to find them, and when we did, we had to take a couple of seconds to take in what we were seeing. They were lying in a small section of hard gravel, an open space between a large collection of piping with gauges and some kind of corrugated tin-roofed office. The best that I could tell was that they were trying to flee when large parts of the crane structure landed on them and then bounced off. They were violently smashed by an unthinkable amount of weight, yet neither body was trapped under anything.

The first victim was face down, his head having been crushed almost flat. His brain had been shot out of the top of his cranium, and it created a fan pattern of gray matter that we had to do our best to avoid. The massive steel structure had the same effect on him as when a human stomps on a ketchup pack.

As if possible, the second victim was even more destroyed. He was found face up, a few feet from his coworker. His rib cage and spine had somehow been smashed out of the left side of his chest cavity, to the point that they lay completely outside of the body to his left, the spine still connected at the lumbar region. His head, arms, and what was left of his chest cavity were to the right in a somewhat normal position. Almost as if the remains were that of a skeleton trying to shed a diver's wet suit.

We were tasked to locate, give first aid, and extricate the victims for transport to the hospital as needed. For these two poor fellows, all we could do for the time being was find their IDs and report back. While going through their pockets, I clearly remember thinking about how sad it was going to be for the supervisor to make phone calls to these guy's families. That was a task I did not envy.

Greens Bayou

To be honest, this call was difficult to get started on paper. The loss of this innocent life and the way it happened is one of the hundreds of memories I don't really like to revisit. Most scenes are very loud and somewhat filled with various other events and distractions. The stillness and lack of chaos at this scene was strange, even in my memory.

We were called to a car in the bayou during one of Houston's many severe thunderstorms that flood the ditches and bayous across the city. This one happened to be about half a mile down the street from Station 64. We arrived on the rescue truck, and the only other units there were Engine 64 and our rescue chief. We were told that a car with five children in it was somewhere under the dark-brown, churning floodwaters of the bayou.

I asked the chief quietly if he said *five* children. He answered yes in a very somber manner, explaining that the story so far was that the uncle and another adult were in the front of the car and got out. There were conflicting stories on how much effort went towards getting the children out, but the end result was that the adults lived, and all five of the children died.

Because of the muddy nature and the level of the floodwaters, we could only guess exactly where the car came to a stop in the bayou. About twenty yards down from the road, I noticed a "pillowing" effect in the water, as if there was a large boulder under the surface. Having lived in a river town for decades and having spent time diving, swimming, kayaking, and just observing the rivers, I almost automatically notice such things. I pointed to the spot and told my captain that I believed that the car was right there. He studied it and agreed. Later, when the water receded, we were proven correct.

Earlier I said that the scene lacked many of the distractions and much of the chaos usually found at scenes. It was muddy, but since the streets were flooding around town, there was very little traffic on the road, therefore not much road noise. The ladder truck and rescue truck were not parked very close, so their diesel engines did not produce the usual background noise. Down on the water's edge, you could only really hear the water, and since the bayou flowed through a grassy field with trees, it was almost peaceful, if not for the tragedy just below the surface. I just remember thinking how surreal it felt.

I talked to several guys from 64's all these years later, including one friend who was with the crew who, the next day, found one of the small children on the bank about a quarter of a mile down. We all still remembered it clearly and just shook our heads.

Double DOA

Extrications can be simply popping open a door that is jammed from a minor fender bender, or basically cutting the vehicle away from the victim as if they were inside a beer can when it was crushed. This next story is more like the latter.

We were dispatched to a motor-vehicle accident with two victims on 288 South. We learned on the way over that the victims were deceased, and the ladder-truck captain on the scene called for us to assist in removing the victims from the vehicle. This, in and of itself, is not an uncommon call. It takes a very long time to extricate bodies from vehicles that have been really crushed. The longer it takes, the longer the highway is backed up, and the longer your firefighters are out in the middle of the highway, which can be less than ideal. This run sticks out in my memory because of the presentation of one of the victims.

Two girls in their early twenties or so appeared to be coming back from a day at the beach. Highway 288 leads out of Houston to Surfside Beach, which is a popular place to spend the day. They were in a small economy car and smashed at full speed into the back of an eighteen-wheeler stopped in front of them, if I remember correctly. In any case, the front of the vehicle was crushed, with major intrusion into the front-seat area.

Both of these poor girls were mangled and crushed by the dashboard in the most destructive manner, but what stood out to me is that upon impact, the girl in the passenger seat must have been sitting with her legs crossed. The force from her knees hitting the dash fractured both of her femur bones and sent the broken, sharp edges straight up through the skin. It looked as if she had two broken, jagged PVC pipes sticking out of her thighs.

You see these things—things that are so far from normal —and all you can do is say a prayer while you continue to do your job.

Chapter 9

28's

I tested for promotion to the rank of E/O. It used to be called "chauffeur," and hearing guys use that term is still very common.

There were no openings on any rescue apparatus for a fresh E/O with zero seniority, so my fate was going the way of the majority of freshly promoted E/Os and leading to driving an ambulance. But not just any ambulance awaited me—Ambulance 528 became my new chariot.

Station 28 was historically one of the top-three busiest stations in the entire city. Sometimes reigning at number one and other years falling to second or third place. Truth be told, once an ambulance starts averaging fifteen or more calls in twenty-four hours, it really doesn't matter if your box makes three or four more calls than the next box—they are both miserable assignments. Many ambulances and stations in the city that were traditionally "not that bad" became as bad or worse almost overnight after Hurricane Katrina. But I think it is fair to say that Ambulance 28 and Ambulance 528 are still on nobody's list of first-choice ambulances.

I was assigned to 28's for almost a year before I was able to pick Ambulance 41; in that time, I never got one night's sleep. NOT ONE SINGLE NIGHT was I able to catch more than a half-hour nap—not once. I was up and going the entire twenty-four-hour shift, every shift, and this was with two ambulances in the same station.

Having been on the rescue truck for the prior three years, I had honestly kind of forgotten what running all night, every shift, was like. Sure, on Rescue 11, we made fires and car wrecks in the middle of the night, but many nights we also slept all night.

I was a complete zombie after my twenty-four-hour shift on Ambulance 28. Thinking back on it makes me laugh because I remember being a rookie, fighting an apartment fire all night long, and getting up and going to play eighteen holes of golf in the morning with little or no ill effects. Well, not anymore.

Back in the day, I could drive in from Canyon Lake, to the house of my buddy Josh, at around midnight. My boys were little guys, and I didn't want to leave until after they had gone to bed. Then I arose at 5:00 a.m., got to 28's by six or so, and worked until six thirty the next day, if I had made it back to the station by then. Not making it back to the station to be relieved at six thirty was a regular occurrence.

If the boys had a school performance, game, or any other kind of event going on, I drove home the next day, tried to take a nap, and then repeated the process of driving in late and getting beat up by the ambulance for another twenty-four hours.

One might ask why I chose to live so far away from where I worked. And I understand. I did not have to live in Canyon Lake and work in Houston. I chose to do this because, at the time, Houston Fire was the best option in terms of pay, benefits, and retirement, and I simply was not willing to uproot my family from the Texas Hill Country and trade raising my sons in the rivers and hills for the streets of Houston. So it was a trade-off I was willing to make, but that doesn't change the fact that I look back on these years of my career as being the hardest.

A Different Side of Town

I was used to working in the parts of Houston that were populated with the poor and lower-income, working-class citizens. The Galleria area had some of those as well, but it also had very wealthy neighborhoods, shopping, dining, and hotels that the very wealthy patronized. A very non-stop, busy district, but also a very interesting one to work. One call that comes to mind was in a particularly expensive and swanky hotel.

We arrived in the hotel room to see HPD already on scene, an older man sitting in a chair and smoking a cigarette, and a very deceased young woman lying in the bed. Because of the blood pooling in her body and the rigor mortis that had already set in, there was no use in trying to resuscitate her after checking for pulses. She had been deceased for hours.

The older "gentleman" was mumbling to himself when we asked what happened. He was honest, at least, and admitted she was a call girl. They had partied with cocaine a little too much, and when he woke up, she was in the state that we observed her in. He then proceeded to look at the cop who was filling out paperwork and asked, "What am I going to tell my wife?"

Good question…

Always Check

At Station 28, on one of the many Highway 59 car wrecks we responded to, we were walking back to the pumper, which was blocking the innermost lane and shoulder. The wreck itself was minor, and there were no serious injuries. One of the guys looked down to the grime-covered shoulder and saw an owner's manual from some car, along with all of the other debris that usually litters a busy highway. For some reason, he bent down and opened it up; in the inside sleeve were two one-hundred-dollar bills!

There were five of us on the truck that day, so we each got forty dollars. Since then, if I see anything similar on the street, I check just to make sure.

"Is This Some Kind of Prank?"

There is one call I will absolutely never forget working at Station 28. As I have stated before, the Galleria area of Houston is different from the rest of the city.

We ran on a sick call to an expensive high-rise apartment building. Squad 3 was already on scene when we stepped off the elevator and into the apartment. Talking to Squad 3 while lying on the couch was a very beautiful woman in very skimpy lingerie. I looked at my partner, he looked at me, and I asked, "Is this some kind of prank with a hidden camera or something?"

The woman said she felt feverish and wanted to go to the hospital. As the medics were talking to her, I noticed on the table was an award from *Playboy* magazine, and on the wall were a couple of framed cover photos from *Playboy* as well. I looked at the photo and looked at her; there was no doubt that at one time she was a Playboy bunny.

We got her a robe to cover up with and loaded her onto the stretcher. As this was a basic call, I told the squad that they could cut loose. For some reason, unlike on every other call, the squad decided to hang out with us until we transported her to the hospital.

"We Was Hoopin'"

We got a call from a high school once for a young man complaining of leg pain. We found him sitting on the ground of the basketball court, and I asked him what was going on.

He responded that he was having sharp pain in the fronts of his legs, just above the ankles—the classic shin-splint area. So I asked him what he was doing when the pain started, and he replied, "We was hoopin'." For those who may not know, that is slang for playing basketball.

We loaded him up in the ambulance and headed for the ER. When we wheeled him up to the triage desk, the nurse interviewed the patient while we were taking a set of vital signs. The golden question was asked again by the nurse. She got the same response—"We was hoopin'." The nurse looked at him and asked him to repeat himself, and the same reply was given. She looked at me, and I explained that they were playing basketball.

Oh, the Irony

We made a stabbing in an apartment complex one night, and it turned out that the victim was a newly arrived illegal immigrant; he was stabbed by another illegal immigrant who had been here a while, had learned some

English, and had some clientele lined up. Well, the newly arrived immigrant underbid the guy who had been here a while and could charge higher prices. So the established immigrant found out who underbid him, and he tried his best to either get rid of the competition or scare him away.

Another time, we picked up an illegal immigrant who had jumped into a concrete bayou with bare feet to get away from being beaten up for the exact same reason. He landed on broken glass, which proceeded to slice his feet to pieces. He was new to the country, would do the same work for less money, and had underbid workers who had been here a while.

"I'm Still So Drunk"

The second formal complaint against me by a citizen happened on the very last call after a typical twenty-four-hour shift on A528. The incident occurred right before shift change, which was 6:30 a.m., and we, as on every shift, had been running all night. While trying to get back to the station, we caught another sick call.

We pulled up to the apartment at the same time the patients were walking down from the second story. A woman's boyfriend was helping her descend the stairs. When she saw us walk up, she said in a very loud voice, "I'm still soooo drunk."

I admit it. I was completely exhausted, and so was my partner. I had reached my bullshit limit for the day. I asked the boyfriend if he was drunk, and he said no. I then asked the drunk female why she hadn't asked her boyfriend to drive her to the ER instead of calling 911.

Well, that set her off, and she screamed, "Thanks for caring about me so much! Really nice attitude!!" My partner started laughing, and that only made her angrier. She reversed back up the stairs—without any help this time— yelling all kinds of stuff I don't remember and telling us to go away.

Okay. No problem, lady.

Before we could get back to the station, dispatch told us to call supervisor 16 when we returned to quarters. The drunk lady had called and complained that fast.

Well, I called a buddy of mine who worked at 16's to get the lowdown on that supervisor and to tell him what happened. He said that the supervisor was a good dude and not to worry. I also told my partner that I would write the report and take all of the heat for anything that came down from higher up. I simply did not care.

So I called supervisor 16 and told him what happened. He told me to make sure and document the fact that she admitted to being drunk, which I had planned to do anyway.

So in my official report, I clearly documented that the patient appeared intoxicated in movement, sounded intoxicated in speech and behavior, and loudly stated that she was very intoxicated. I never heard anything else about it. The fact that she admitted to being drunk meant that no other statement she made could possibly be reliable.

Chapter 10

On to 41's

In reality, there is no good ambulance in the city of Houston anymore. There are a few still left that are not as busy as others, but if we are talking the difference between two and four runs over twenty-four hours, then they are all pretty much the same.

In my opinion, it is the runs after midnight that make or break being on an ambulance. In the year I was assigned to Ambulance 528, we never—not one time—had a night that we did not run all night. Not once. I clearly remember praying and saying, "Lord, just let me get two hours of sleep tonight so I am not so tired driving home." It never happened.

So when openings came up for other ambulances around town, I naturally looked to see what was available, as I did not have enough seniority as an E/O yet to get even a busy pumper truck. A41 on the D shift came open, and the captain was a friend of mine from 77's.

A41 was not a great box by any standard, but after talking to a couple of guys from 41's, I learned that the box will have some bad nights and some pretty good nights of only one or two runs after midnight. So, hoping for the best, I put in for A41 and got it.

It turned out to be a good choice as I worked with some of my career's favorite team members at Station 41 with HFD.

Ambulance 41 and Coke Street

By this time in my career, I had made so many EMS calls that besides the ones that stand out in my memory, they all just seem to blend together into one big sleep-deprived gumbo. Station 41 is a small house that serves a historically Black neighborhood called Pleasantville. It is also right outside of the Fifth Ward, Denver Harbor, and on the Houston Ship Channel. At least half of my daily calls were in The Nickel (the Fifth Ward), the majority of which were to a set of apartments located on Coke Street.

There are many locations and addresses that Houston firemen have burned into their memories—1919 Runnels, Banjo and Little York, Antoine and Desoto, Gulfton Ghettos, 1811 Ruiz Street (Star of Hope Mission), just to name a few. But the apartments on Coke Street deserve their own paragraph. I used to say that if I let go of my steering wheel, the box could drive itself to the apartments on Coke Street that were much visited by HFD and HPD.

I clearly remember many times making runs there and seeing Station 19 on scene at one apartment and Station 27 on scene on the other side of the complex while we were making a call to one of the other apartments. Three Houston fire stations tied up in one apartment complex that, honestly, was not a huge complex by Houston standards.

This was several years ago, and I have heard parts of the area are becoming gentrified and nicer places to live. I even heard that the apartments there have been remodeled in an effort to make them nicer. I hope that is true, but when I was assigned to Ambulance 41 around 2010, it was a hotbed of 911 calls, to put it nicely.

Neglect

A call during my time on A41 that stands out in my memory was to an elderly Hispanic woman in the Denver Harbor area. Denver Harbor is the traditionally Hispanic neighborhood right across the railroad tracks from the Fifth Ward. The call came in as leg pain or something of that nature, and upon arrival, we found an elderly grandmother sitting on her couch. She spoke no English, so her grandson was there translating for us.

We narrowed down her pain complaint to her feet, and when we took off her slippers, I simply could not believe what we saw. Her toenails on both feet were so long that they curled to the bottoms of her feet and were causing her pain when she walked. Each toenail had to be six inches long or more.

I looked at the twenty-something grandson and asked who was in charge of taking care of her. He said he and his uncle. I responded by asking how they never noticed this because it takes a very long time to get in that condition. At this question, he got very defensive, started saying stuff about how I was accusing him of not loving his dear "*abuelita*," and began posturing as if he wanted to fight. I calmly told him that fighting a member of HFD was a road he didn't want to go down, and this made him posture even more into his vato-loco act that he was trying to put on. We loaded the elderly woman onto the stretcher while he kept repeating, "What are you trying to say, *ese*?"

While removing her from the house, all five foot four of him actually got in my way and tried to "bow up" on me. I calmly got right back in his face and told him he needed to move. The medic from the squad got between us and informed the kid that he would be going to jail and facing a big fine for attacking a member of HFD.

HPD arrived on scene, and I let them look at the poor neglected lady's feet and then left them to talk to the tough guy who can't take care of Grandma.

Barking Mad

In 41's territory, there was a house that called 911 at least once every shift. Anyone who has worked at 41's any length of time has made her and knows exactly who I am talking about. Her house was across the tracks and on the left. She was a drunk, and sometimes we were called for her elderly parent when she clearly just wanted out of the house so she could party. All of her calls seem to blend together, except for one time when she was drunk, high, or both, and more than likely possessed by a demonic spirit, in my opinion.

As soon as we entered the house as usual, she got down on all fours and started crawling around, barking and growling. The growl was not some fake human growl as if someone is trying to imitate a dog. This was an actual deep growl coming out of this woman as she crawled closer to me and barked with insane-looking eyes. I got myself ready to kick her into the next room if she tried to bite me.

I seem to recall that the call wasn't even for her, but for someone else there who was having chest pains, because I don't remember loading her into the ambulance at this particular time. Being drunk at home and acting like an idiot is not against the law, and she was not the patient with a chief complaint. She was, however, even in the privacy of her own home, proving that she was a complete drain on society and contributing nothing.

Scammers

There have been scammers, grifters, and cons throughout human history, and, believe it or not, the 911 caller in "need" is no exception. I made a call to the pack-rat house of a hoarder once. You could barely move without bumping into and knocking over a pile of junk. While carrying my jump bag out, which is not small, the bag hit a punch bowl, and it shattered on the floor.

The lady called HFD and claimed it was some priceless antique bowl worth thousands. A chief downtown finally got ahold of me and asked what happened. I told him that, yes, I did knock down her bowl, and it shattered, so this lady wasn't lying. We talked a little more about the call, and I asked him if I was going to be held personally responsible for the bowl. He said not to worry about it, and I never heard about it again.

In our conversation, the chief said HFD gets dozens of claims per week of firefighters supposedly causing damage and people wanting money in return. He even said that people try claiming that HFD personnel have stolen items from their homes, and they want restitution. Of course, all of these items are always said to be worth thousands of dollars.

I admit that I was at first a little surprised at hearing that people try to file claims against the firefighters who are there to take care of them, that they try to ruin the firefighter's career over a few dollars. But then again, why would that surprise me? There are people out there who simply don't care what happens to their fellow man as long as they can benefit even a small amount. Little did I know that I would be accused of thievery at the scene of a car wreck just a few years later.

My partner that day was a good guy and a good EMT, and we usually got along well together. He was a believer, and we had several conversations about church and the Bible. We were called to a motor-vehicle accident late one evening on the north side of the Ship Channel Bridge, about a hundred yards from where the bridge meets land again. It was raining and the northbound car had been coming off the bridge, probably going too fast, and it slid off the road and into the tall, thick salt grass and bushes on the side of the road.

HPD and wrecker trucks were already on scene when we arrived, and we waded out through the wet weeds to assess the patient. There were large, deep ruts in the soft, muddy ground; they ran from the roadway to where he stopped, but there was not much actual damage to the car. The driver seemed to be more concerned with gathering belongings in the car than with any injuries.

We interviewed him, and he wanted to go to the hospital to get checked anyway, which was fine with us. Transport to the hospital was much easier at this hour than waking up a supervisor and getting a non-transport signature. Pretty routine call as far as EMS goes.

The next working day, we were told that we had a complaint filed against us for stealing a gold ring from the center console of the car. A chief from downtown asked each of us about the scene and if we saw a gold ring at any time during the call. Neither of us recalled seeing a ring, and we told the chief what happened on the call, which was nothing. We arrived, assessed, and transported a patient to the ER. The patient kept insisting that there was a gold ring taken by HFD EMS.

Was there ever even a ring in the first place? Who knows, and I don't even know what came of the situation. We gave our statements and never heard about it again. I think the fact that HPD was on the scene and involved may have somehow helped us out, but I'm not sure.

Miscellaneous

As I have stated before, I made so many calls on the ambulance at 41's, and in my career in general, they honestly start to run together. Some, however, just stand out in my memory for some reason or another.

Once, there was an arsonist breakdancing in the street in front of the house he set on fire.

We made a scene in which the mom approached and begged us to get HPD to stop abusing her "baby boy." Her "baby boy" was a full-grown man, with weed and gang tattoos, who decided he wanted to fight the cops.

So many calls to apartments—not just at 41's, but at every station I worked—in which small children were up at 2:00 a.m. or later, running around on school nights as if that were just normal.

The chance to take the ARFF class came up, and even though I had never thought about going out to the airport before, the opportunity to be at a slow station in which I could study for captain sounded as if it was just what I needed.

Chapter 11

Bush IAH

After taking the ARFF (aircraft-rescue firefighting course) and getting my state certification, I had to wait for an opening that I had enough time and points to lock in. It was a few months later when I returned from a call, and my captain told me that postings came out and that I got an ARFF spot at Bush Airport. I told him to stop playing with me because I knew two other guys with more seniority than I had who were putting in for the same spots. He said that he wasn't joking and handed me the posting to see for myself. The other two were not allowed to transfer from their current spots for reasons I honestly don't remember, but for me, it was a good day.

ARFF Slug

That is the reputation that ARFF firefighters have on the streets. A bunch of fat, lazy slugs that don't want to move or make fires anymore. As with anything in life, there is always a mixture of truth and exaggeration. Were there slugs at ARFF? For sure, but also there are slugs at regular fire stations all over the city. And to be truthful with the reader, I don't care if I make another house fire or working apartment fire ever again. I have been to dozens of full-blown working fires in my career, and at several, I was the first one in the door with the nozzle. And besides the short-lived adrenaline rush and satisfaction of putting out an active fire, it sucks. A working house fire is maybe twenty minutes of go time and then hours of dirty, unhealthy grunt work in an environment that is not ideal. I have been there and done that enough times to say that I don't care anymore about "making fires." If it happens, then let's go take care of business and help people, but my days of wanting to fight fire are long gone.

Except for wildland/brush fires. For some reason, I still enjoy wildland firefighting, even though it can be more manual labor and a longer duration than a house fire.

ARFF Runs

Because of the nature of the calls at the airport, there were not too many memorable runs that deserve to be put down in a memoir. Most of the calls were to line the runway with the crash trucks when any airplane has had a warning light come on for low tire pressure, a bird strike, a smell of smoke on the plane, or for any other reasons the pilot may deem necessary. For the most part, the airplanes land safely, and we follow them to the gate just as a precaution, and that is a good thing. If there were a plane crash, dozens and dozens of people would die often. Thank the Lord that is not the case.

But we did have a few engine fires and flat tires, and even had a Cessna catch fire on the taxiway. The entire plane burned by the time the ARFF trucks got there to put it out.

We ran EMS calls to the terminals and gates and had several CPR sessions on the plane, in the jetway, and in the terminals, and many times we had to get people out of stuck parking-garage elevators.

Nose, Gear Up

The aircraft emergency that came closest to a catastrophe that I responded to was a "nose landing, gear up." Technically it was an airplane crash, and this is a fact I had to remind the passengers of when they wanted to go back on the airplane and get their bags. As an aviation crash landing, the plane and everything on it was under investigation until the cause was determined, and/or the contents of the plane were released by the investigative authority.

An Embraer 175 (similar to a small Boeing 737) contacted the tower, saying they could not get confirmation that their nose gear was all the way deployed, so they requested a tower flyby so the tower could visually inspect with binoculars if the front landing gear was indeed down or not.

The plane flew by, and it was confirmed that the gear was not deployed, so the aircraft went into a circular flight pattern around the airport to try and figure out what to do. After several unsuccessful attempts to fix the situation, an emergency was declared, and we were dispatched to line runway 9-27 for a confirmed nose landing, gear up.

This was an emergency that pilots train for, but knowing that we were about to witness and respond to a possible real plane crash was somewhat unnerving, to say the least. I was driving the pumper at this time and not a crash truck, so we were a crew of four on the truck. After crossing the airfield to reach our response position, and waiting for the plane's final approach, one of the guys in the back offered up a prayer to the Lord for the safety of the crew and passengers on board the plane.

Eventually, the plane came in for landing, and I remember watching with fascination as the rear wheels touched down, the plane rolled in the wheelie position as long as it could, and then the nose of the fuselage finally came down on the pavement. Being that it was in the evening, not in bright sunshine, the visibility of the shower of sparks coming up both sides of the jet lit up the runway like a fireworks show. The plane slid under its shower of sparks for several hundred yards and then came to a stop.

Crash trucks pulled up and immediately began to spray the nose section area with water and foam. Then the emergency chutes were pulled, and the yellow life-raft-looking slides deployed out of the front and rear of the plane. I didn't see it, but we were told later that one of the flight attendants was completely drenched by one of the crash truck's water patterns and knocked off their feet. Later, on the thermal-imaging camera, we did see a very portly flight attendant slide down the rear slide, bounce at the bottom of the slide, and land on the pavement below like a giant human water balloon. It was so funny that we rewound and watched that footage several times.

The passengers started pouring off the plane, and it was our job to direct them to one spot near the pumper so we could keep them out of the way of firefighting and rescue efforts and start accounting for all passengers. Well, this was much more difficult than it sounds, as almost every passenger immediately turned around to face the plane and started to record with their cell phones. Passengers wandered off in every direction but where they were supposed to go, and we had to yell and round them up as best we could.

After the flight attendants did their checks and declared all passengers were off the plane, we moved the crowd away from the wreck as they waited for transport to arrive. Some of the passengers started to complain that they were not allowed back on the plane to get their carry-on bags. So many, in fact, that I had to loudly get their attention and remind them that they had just survived an actual plane crash due to the expertise and cool hands of their pilot and that maybe they should think about that. This seemed to bring them back to reality for at least a little while.

The comment about the skill of the pilot and the credit he deserves is warranted. The nose of the plane was less than a foot away from the runway centerline after it was all said and done. He kept that plane going straight down the runway, even while sliding on the belly of the fuselage.

Chapter 12

Looking Back

I suppose the tendency to look back on decisions you have made in life, and to evaluate whether or not those decisions ended in a net positive or net negative, is a normal human quality. I don't dwell on mistakes made in the past, but I am also honest enough to admit that maybe some decisions were better than others.

I look back on my career in the fire service thus far, and overall I feel it was a positive experience, mainly because of all of the time I got to spend with my family. I put out house fires, extricated people from terrible car wrecks, and helped people on the worst days of their lives. And I feel I did it with a sense of duty and honor worthy of the profession.

I love the traditions, the uniform, and the bagpipes and drums playing, but all of that is secondary to having had so much time with my sons. The sleepless nights, dangerous situations, and the bureaucracy that comes with being a city employee at the mercy of a mayor who may or may not like the fire department were all worth it because I got so many days off with my boys.

When I look back, the overall feeling I get can be boiled down to one word really—"tired." So tired that sometimes I really don't know how it all worked out. For a few years on the box, I went into the station to sleep the night before, but the alarm went off all night and kept me up, making it seem as though I had started my shift behind the eight ball already.

I was very conscious of not letting this adversely affect my job performance, and I think if you ask anyone who worked with me, they will agree that I was a quality HFD employee who performed his job properly. But, with regret, I have to admit that being so tired made me irritable. During this period of my career, my patience level was probably not something to be admired.

And yes, I admit that refusing to move back to Houston was my own choice; I never stated anything to the contrary. I just simply was not going to uproot my kids from Canyon Lake/New Braunfels and raise them in Houston, all things considered. I am glad I stuck it out.

Opinions on 911 EMS System

In one word—broken. I'm not saying it doesn't function at all, because most of the time when someone dials 911, a firetruck or ambulance will show up and handle the situation. I am saying it is broken because of the abuse and misuse of the so-called "emergency" 911 system and the fact that cities just allow the abuse of the system to continue with impunity.

I have had many firefighters in the past say that abuse of the 911 system is "job security." I reject that on the basis that there will always be actual emergencies that need to be taken care of, so the job of the first responder will never go away.

So what can be done? Well, fire departments can lobby legislatures around the country to help with completely frivolous lawsuits that cities are so scared to fight. Cities and departments are so scared of litigation that we are told to just transport anyone and everyone who wants it. If that is the endgame, then just take *E* off EMS and call it a medical taxi service.

But, truth be told, that hope is probably unrealistic. But I will keep fighting the good fight and holding on to the idealism that seems to guide my thoughts and beliefs. After all, if you let that optimism slip away, then all is truly lost. And I refuse to give in to that.

Postscript

I would be remiss to not thank coworkers and friends:

Anthony for the sound advice, friendship, and hours of conversations.

Jason D. for being a good guy and helping my son's racing career.

Natty P. for making me think and dig deeper.

Javier and Jafet for the español and Karl for the music jams.

Jackie H. and Johnny B. for the calm perspectives on a variety of issues.

Aaron C., Andy B., Dennis, Salty, and 54A's crew for accommodating me on my middle days.

Tony, Mike, and Jason F. for being the best engine crew I was ever a part of.

Chief C. and Chief R. for honest talks about issues.

Ricky B., Matty, C-Money Mason, and all of 54B's crew (Dusty, Chap, Brian, Noack, Ronnie D., and Rogers) for being good people and solving the world's problems around the table.

Zayne for the smoked queso.

Ralphie, Owens, Hoffy, Captain Holmes and the rest of 54D.

Foster S., Super Dave, Ryan L., and Sam C. for being good people.

B.J. for the laughter and Jerry W. for being the best senior FF I ever had.

J.D. and Ken F. for being good captains and good men.

Ryan J. and Jerry Love for the laughter.

Cody C. for the hunts.

Darren B., Clint, Robert S., Obuch, and Robert G. for the friendship over the years.

Bucky, Chief Z., and Bill for years of friendship also.

My new crew, Pom, Mikey, Greg and Cristian.

King-Davis for that heartfelt announcement at my retirement.

I know I have probably left people out, and for that, I apologize. It seems almost impossible to list everyone who has had a positive impact on me. I encourage everyone to write your stories down as well so your grandchildren and beyond can know what you did. Too much is lost to the next generations.

About Joel Simmons

Get to know Joel Simmons.

Email: akindface73@gmail.com

Printed in the USA
CPSIA information can be obtained
at www.ICGtesting.com
LVHW010837280524
781470LV00002B/272